MW01136693

REMOTE

THE FIVE

BOOKS BY ERIC RICKSTAD

THE REMOTE SERIES
Remote: The Six
Remote: The Five

THE CANAAN CRIME SERIES
The Silent Girls
Lie in Wait
The Names of Dead Girls

STANDALONE NOVELS
Lilith
I Am Not Who You Think I Am
What Remains of Her
Reap

ERIC RICKSTAD

REMOTE
THE FIVE

BLACK STONE
PUBLISHING

Copyright © 2025 by Eric Rickstad
Published in 2025 by Blackstone Publishing
Cover and book design by Candice Edwards

The characters and events in this book are fictitious.
Any similarity to real persons, living or dead, is coincidental
and not intended by the author.

Printed in the United States of America

First edition: 2025
ISBN 978-1-0940-0063-3
Thrillers / Crime

Version 1

Blackstone Publishing
31 Mistletoe Rd.
Ashland, OR 97520

www.BlackstonePublishing.com

REMOTE

THE FIVE

CHAPTER 1

She watches the man take cash from his slim billfold as he banters with the cashier. He shakes his head and laughs at something the cashier says. With his effete manner and his diminutive stature and his peach ascot, he gives no suggestion of any sinister intent. He is charming and debonair and moves about the world with aplomb and a jocularity that makes those he engages feel themselves a part of his good-naturedness.

The man steps aside to await his order, speaking to a plump middle-aged woman beside him. Within seconds, the woman is laughing with the man, touching his elbow with her fingers.

He's that sort of man, and also another sort. A sort not visible here, in the public realm.

His name is John Randolph, and now he takes from the end of the counter his coffee and a brown waxed-paper bag that she knows contains a wedge of poppy-seed cake.

He heads toward the door, saying, "Excuse me, pardon me" as he pushes through the crush of patrons, a couple times touching the shoulders of women with his fingertips as he makes his way, smiling, coming toward the door, toward her.

She puts on a bucket hat and pulls it down low, follows him outside into the raw, wet day, her breath pluming in the cold air.

Randolph walks down the sidewalk, tapping his cane with one hand as he sips his coffee, the bag with the cake in it tucked into the pocket of his Barbour coat.

As he strolls along, he peeks into the shop windows, subtly preening his hair and adjusting his ascot in a manner that betrays he's not window-shopping or looking with curiosity at displays of goods.

She remains a half block behind the man, herself looking into shop windows, her hand tucked inside her coat pocket, gripping the knife.

Randolph walks around the corner, out of sight. She doesn't step up her pace. She knows where he is headed.

When she comes around the corner, she sees him standing at the crosswalk waiting for the light, his car fob out.

The light changes and he skips across the street, brandishing his fob and pressing it.

The lights of an Audi sedan flash as the car beeps twice.

Randolph approaches it.

She remains on the far side of the street.

When he gets into the Audi, she crosses the street to the parking lot, awaiting the sound she knows is coming.

The Audi fires up, stutters, and dies.

She waits at the edge of the lot.

The sound comes again.

The next time, the engine doesn't fire at all. It gives a weak gasp and dies.

For a minute, no sound comes, but by the look of Randolph inside the car, he is turning the key in the ignition, hunched over the wheel as if to encourage the engine.

This is her cue. She wanders over, in front of the Audi. She is halfway across the front of his hood when he looks up from the driver's seat. His face is flushed.

She smiles.

Randolph does not smile. He bows his head again and works the key. Being this close, she can hear a tiny *click click click* from the engine.

She smiles to herself.

Randolph pounds the steering wheel with his palm. She hears another sound—*clack*. The Audi's hood pops open.

He gets out and strides to the front of the car. He wedges a finger under the lip of the hood and feels around for the latch.

"*Heck!*" he says, and yanks his hand away, sucking on a finger.

He notices her standing beside the car next to his, her keys out.

"Car troubles?" she says.

Randolph gains his composure, shoulders shivering like those of a bird in the rain.

He gives her a querulous look.

"It happens," she says.

He glowers. "Not to me." He is deflated of all the charm he exhibited in the café. He is the sort of man whose easy ebullience lasts as long as things go his way. When things don't go his way, his veneer is stripped raw to expose his impatience and anger and need for control.

She takes out her phone and feigns looking at the screen. "Want me to get a tow truck?" she says. "This app my brother forced me to get works like a charm."

"What I need is an Uber or a cab—a ride," Randolph says. "I've a seminar in Vail, and if not for my addiction to poppy-seed cake, I'd have plenty of time, but alas . . ."

"Ooh. The poppy-seed cake?" She beams and produces a brown paper bag from her purse. "From Kaffeeklatsch? It's just the best, isn't it?"

Randolph smiles. "Calling it the best makes it sound like it has competition," he says. "When we know it does not."

"An Uber or cab isn't going to drive you way out to Vail—not without it costing a fortune." She smiles as her mouth goes dry. "I'll drive you."

Randolph squints at her. She realizes now how queer an offer it is for a woman to make to a strange man.

"My car's a mess," she says. "Nothing fancy like yours. But if you can stand it, I'm going out that way for a wedding at the Sonnenalp."

The mention of the tony hotel seems to disarm the man.

He pulls back his coat sleeve, looks at his gold wristwatch. He looks at her.

"What can it hurt?" he says.

———

Randolph sits in the back seat of her car.

She didn't expect this. It's a wrinkle. Why would he sit in the back, as if she were his driver? Perhaps he doesn't want to sit up front with a woman he doesn't know, does not want to give any impression of seeking physical closeness. Or he's used to being chauffeured.

"You can sit up front," she says. "I don't bite."

"I didn't know where you'd prefer me. I'm a stranger to you."

"You don't look like you bite either."

"Only poppy-seed cake."

"Sit wherever you prefer," she says.

Randolph gets out and sits in the front seat. He buckles up, placing a laptop bag at his feet and clutching the bag with the poppy-seed cake on his lap.

As she drives, he takes a napkin out of the bag and unfolds it on his lap. He takes out the poppy-seed cake and bites off a hunk, places the rest of the cake on the napkin, and rubs the crumbs free of his fingertips with his thumb. He works his mouth, chewing. "Mmm, darn good cake." He sips his coffee. "Better when the coffee is still hot, but I'll take it." He scarfs up the cake, gluttonous. A few more bites, and it's gone.

"You really like that cake."

"It's special cake."

She nods at her bag with the cake in it. "Have mine too," she says.

"I couldn't possibly."

"Of course you could. I can grab a piece anytime. I live here."

He eyes the bag. "You sure?"

"Help yourself. I want you to have it. It's special cake, after all."

"Obliged."

He takes a big bite out of the cake. Washes it down with coffee. In a minute, the cake is gone.

She merges into the right lane to take the exit ramp.

For a moment, Randolph, busy collecting crumbs of cake with a press of his thumb, doesn't notice. Only as the car slows and she navigates the long curve of the ramp does he pay attention. She feels his eyes on her but keeps her own eyes straight ahead.

"What are you doing?" There is an edge of unease in his voice. He is the type of man who ought to take every precaution but didn't. Against his best interests, he didn't.

She glances at the fuel gauge. "I didn't realize I was so low on gas. I need to fill up."

The man stretches his neck out, peers at the dash.

The fuel gauge is low. Of course it is low. She made sure of it.

Just as she made sure the poppy-seed cake she gave him was special.

Randolph glances at his watch, twitchy. He takes out his cell phone. "I need to let them know I might be late," he says.

"I'll get you there on time. It won't take long to gas up."

"My time is already tight. The people I'm going to see are not forgiving. They don't tolerate tardiness."

"It sounds important."

"In its way."

"Sounds like *you're* important," she says.

Randolph snorts. "In certain circles, a person is only as valuable as his knowledge. Not even that, but how much knowledge they are willing to *share* with you."

She knows this. She knows everything she needs to know about this John Ellard Randolph, and much she doesn't need to know.

"What is it you do, if you don't mind my asking?" she says.

"I'm a . . . philanthropist, of a sort. I fund research."

"Must be important research if you're going all the way to Vail to give a lecture," she says.

"I believe it to be."

"What sort of research?"

"All the cake in the world can't get me to divulge that."

"In general, nothing specific."

"We need to get fueled up as fast as possible. I really must arrive on time for the cocktail party. This ilk love to schmooze. I'd prefer to read a book in my room, but such is the world."

He works his thumbs on his phone screen.

"How are there no bars here?" He glares out his window as if the answer were out there somewhere amid the sage.

"We're not exactly in New York City," she says.

"Why can't I get service? What's going on? There are always at least three bars, even out here. Without exception. Always."

She takes her phone from her coat pocket. "No bars on mine either."

"I don't care about your phone," he snaps. "I care about mine." His voice is barnacled with contempt. "We'll just have to be quicker now, won't we? Step on it. Get your dear gas and get us back on the dang highway."

"I'll do my best," she says.

"See you do."

She takes a left onto a dirt road.

"What the hell are you doing?" he says. He blinks rapidly, wincing, as if he has sand in his eyes. "This isn't the way . . ." he says. His voice slows.

"That depends on where you're going," she says.

"We're going to . . ." He blinks. "To . . ."

"Yes?"

He smacks his lips, licks them, struggles to swallow, as if he has a mouthful of glue. "This isn't . . . the way," he slurs.

"It is," she says. "You've been heading this way your whole life."

"I don't feel well," he says.

"You *aren't* well."

"There's something wrong." Sweat glistens on his forehead, and when the car hits a bump in the dirt road, he cups his mouth as if he might be sick. "Go back," he says. "We need to go back."

"There is no going back."

"They're waiting for you—I mean, *me*, they're waiting for me."

He works his phone, his fingers dumb. The phone slips from his hand onto the car floor. He stares at it as if trying to determine what this object is.

"And they'll keep waiting," she says.

He sags against the door with a moan, his cheek flat against the window.

"You—did you . . . do something . . ."

"It will wear off."

He eyes her sidelong, unable to lift his head and look at her square.

"Who . . . are you?" he says.

"You know who I am."

He squints at her. He tries to lift his head from the window, but it falls back with a dull thud.

She smiles. "Remember me now? It was a while ago."

"You . . . you were her."

"I am still her."

His eyes close.

He sleeps.

She gets gas at the next town as he sleeps.

Then she drives and drives, for hours and hours, through state after state.

CHAPTER 2

Q tries to glance over his shoulder at his hands cuffed to the chair behind his back, but he can't contort himself that much. He looks around the white laboratory, one of a legion on the Stargazer campus, one he's never been privy to, until now. A window must be open a crack because he can hear the wind whistle, blinds rattle.

Q grins, an ooze of menace spreading across his face.

His eyes meet the watery gray eyes of his *captor*.

His captor does not grin.

"Fools," Q says. "To the very last man. Fools."

All is going according to plan.

Stark gave Q back to the program at Stargazer because he believed this was the worst punishment for him, that the program was where Q least wanted to be, even less than prison itself.

How naive Franklin and Stark had been. When Q understood that there would be no escaping his eventual capture as the Tableau Killer, he'd contrived to be at Stark's house in some faux revenge ploy, as if he cared a lick about the agent's precious wife or their brat. He knew eventually Garnier would remote-view him at Stark's house, and Q and Stark would come running to *save the day.*

Stark believed Q tied up Stark's wife and son because Q is deranged. Q is not deranged. Everything Q does has purpose. He is no Golden State Killer, Boston Strangler, or Jack the Ripper. Q kills not to satisfy a sick personal fetish. His killings have meaning for humankind. What others call "victims" he calls humankind's necessary sacrifices. He takes no pleasure in killing. He does take a measure of pride in knowing that his work will one day be appreciated. Celebrated. He is making history. Shaping it. But there is more to do. Much more. And being back here, on the Stargazer campus, is the best way to do it. If he'd returned voluntarily, he'd have faced suspicion and interrogation, and never be trusted again. He would be no prodigal son. He knew he had to be given back by Franklin and Stark, seemingly *against his will.*

"Can we lose the cuffs? The show is over," Q says. His captor took the cuffs off during most of their nonstop drive west and put them on him again a few miles from the gates and tall fences outside the Stargazer campus.

"We need it to look legitimate," the fool says.

There is no we, Q thinks. "It feels legitimate," he says, and winces to show his discomfort. "You cranked them tight."

A clock on the wall ticks.

"Appearances are important," the fool says.

The fool is taking his time to uncuff him, perhaps enjoying the show a bit too much.

Finally, the fool slips a key from his pocket and stands behind Q.

Q can sense the key going in, hear the soft snick, feel the cuffs relax.

"There," the fool says.

Q rubs his wrists as the fool comes around to face him. "You didn't have to make them so tight," Q says.

The blinds rattle.

Q grunts a violent laugh. "Who arranged all of this with Franklin?"

"I don't know," the fool says. "I told you. I was told to pick you up. I was stationed in that region, so they chose me. You know how it is. I'm a worker bee. The deal with the FBI and the contact in the program is not my concern."

"Who runs the program, Stargazer?" Q says.

"Why the sudden inquisitiveness?"

"Being in the outer world, the Wilds, has made me . . . curious."

"Dr. Romeau tasked me with getting you," the fool finally relents. "I suppose I can tell you now since he'll be here any moment to debrief you."

"Who told Dr. Romeau to task you?"

"Perhaps . . . Dr. Leon?"

"And who told Leon?" Q said.

"I've no idea. I doubt the Man with the White Hair would be bothered with such low-level workings, if that is what you are suggesting. No offense, but you don't rise to the Man with the White Hair's conscious any more than I do."

"You just obey Dr. Romeau." Q takes a step toward him. "As obedient as a beaten dog. Do his bidding. Why didn't Romeau himself fetch me, if I'm so important?"

"Perhaps he had more important matters. They made a mistake letting you leave."

Q laughs. "They didn't let me leave. I escaped. We were prisoners here."

"You shouldn't speak this way. You don't seem the same when you do."

"I'm *not* the same. I learned things out in the Wilds."

"My life is in service of a greater cause, as is yours. Now. We go." The fool reaches for Q.

Q seizes the fool's wrist and cranks it back hard. It cracks. The fool howls with pain.

Q jerks a knee up and breaks the fool's forearm. The fool drops to his knees as Q drives a knee under the fool's chin. His jaw breaks, and he sags to the floor.

Q breaks his neck.

His breathing is labored, and he is sweating.

He hears footsteps out in the hall. He takes hold of the fool's arms and drags his limp body across the lab toward a closet. The door to the lab starts to turn. Q opens the closet door and hauls the body inside and shuts the closet door. He turns to see Dr. Romeau enter the room.

CHAPTER 3

FBI Special Agent Lukas Stark read the text message Agent Jayla King held up to him on her phone.

The message confounded him. Terrified him.

From the look on Gilles Garnier's face, the text had the same impact on him.

"Are you there?" Stark's wife's voice said.

Stark spoke into his phone. "I'm here," he said.

"I thought I lost you," Sarah said.

"I'm here," Stark said. It was all he could think to say.

The text King showed him was from a woman known as S. She was one of the Six remote viewers raised with Garnier in the Stargazer program, a covert government organization where the Six had been raised and trained to harness and hone their innate remote-viewing abilities.

Garnier had recognized S in Agent King's photo. S was suspected of murdering individuals in some belief that the victims could help her revive her remote-viewing ability, which had begun to fail her, as it had Garnier and Q, resulting in debilitating migraines, exhaustion, and nausea.

"What's going on?" Sarah said, her voice still raw from screaming during the violent attack on her and their son, Francis, during which they'd been bound to chairs and nearly murdered by a madman known to the public as the Tableau Killer, and known to Stark and Garnier as Q.

"You seem distracted," Sarah said.

"I'm with some agents," Stark said, his eyes locked on the text.

"At our *house*?" Sarah said. She had made it clear she never wanted to step inside their house, their home, ever again.

"Not inside," Stark said. "Outside."

"When can you get here to pick us up?"

"Soon."

He needed her to know he was here for Francis and her. He needed to pick them up at the hospital and bring them to a safe place he had in mind, where they could begin the long process of recovering from their assault.

"How soon?" Sarah said. "We're being discharged."

"I'm leaving now."

Sarah ended the call without another word.

Agent King was still brandishing her phone screen at Stark. It was difficult to comprehend the full scope of what the text meant.

A car slowed as it drove past the end of Stark's driveway, a blue Camry—his mailman.

"We have to act on this," King said.

"It's your case. You take the reins on it," Stark said. "I can't."

"I don't have the experience," King said. "Or the authority."

The Camry stopped at his mailbox, and an arm came out from the passenger window and opened the box.

"Then back-burner it," Stark said.

"It's high priority. There are lives at risk, sir."

The Camry drove down to the next mailbox, its brakes giving a slight squeak as it stopped.

"There are always lives at risk," Stark said. "My sole priority is my wife and son's safety."

Yet, even as he said it, Stark could not help reading the text once more.

The text made it clear that S was viewing them *right now*—at this very instant. She was watching them. And threatening them.

> It will take more than the three of
> you to stop me.
> Soon, just two of you.

This woman, suspected of the murders of two MIT researchers in the fields of bioengineering and genome modification, had the same strange scar on the back of her neck that Garnier and Q had. This woman whom Garnier suspected of being manipulated by the program, as was Q, into murdering a list of individuals in the hope of maintaining or strengthening their fading remote-viewing abilities. Of course, it might really have been only a test by the program to see how far the two would go to maintain their ability—to determine how strong their addiction to that power really was.

"They're preparing for something," Garnier said.

CHAPTER 4

"Daddy!" Francis yelled as he rushed toward Stark as he entered the hospital room.

Sarah stayed silent.

"Are we going home now?" Francis said to Stark's surprise. Stark hadn't imagined his son would ever want to go home after what had happened to him and his mother there.

"We're going somewhere else," Sarah said, placing a hand on Francis's shoulder.

Francis glanced up at her. "Why?"

"We're going someplace . . . fun," Sarah said.

"Home is fun," Francis said.

Stark tried to hide his astonishment. He had no idea how Francis could describe their home as fun. Not now. Not after the brutality. The terror. It made no sense.

"You're going to a place with horses and a pool and a TV much bigger than ours," Stark said. On the ride to the hospital, he'd called an old colleague who owed him a favor and arranged for Sarah and Francis to stay at a small house in Albemarle.

"Horses? For how long?" Francis said, his face dour.

Sarah looked to Stark for help. But Stark was in disbelief himself at how removed the boy seemed from the violence he had suffered not twenty hours earlier. "For a while," Stark said. "We don't want to go back home right now."

"I do," Francis said.

Did the boy not remember what had happened? Was he repressing it? It would be a natural response to sudden violent trauma, to delay absorbing the reality of it. To remain in denial until the reality struck its blow. Yet it seemed Francis would harbor at least some fear of their home now.

"It will be fun for us to stay at a cabin, sweetie," Sarah said.

"I wanna go home," Francis insisted.

Sarah seemed as mystified and troubled as Stark by their son's response.

"We'll take some time to spoil ourselves and just relax. Maybe you can learn to ride a horse," Sarah said.

"I don't care about dumb horses," Francis said.

Stark's phone rang.

Sarah flinched.

Stark slipped his hand into his pocket.

"Don't," Sarah said.

Stark withdrew his hand.

"Promise we'll only stay at the cabin for a little while? And go back home soon?" Francis said. "All my stuffies are there."

"I brought a couple stuffies with me," Stark said.

"And Daddy will get anything else you need from the house," Sarah said. "If that's why you want to go back." Her frown deepened as Stark took out his phone and looked at it. The call was from Agent King.

"I want my bed. My house," Francis pressed.

"Not *now*," Sarah barked, exasperated as Stark texted Agent King. "Don't argue with me."

CHAPTER 5

Stark and Sarah sat on the front deck of a cabin that had served as a horse trainers' quarters in the early 1900s. It squatted beneath a canopy of black walnut trees on the back forty of a sprawling Southern estate in Albemarle County, an hour outside Charlottesville. The fifth-generation breeding and training farm and stable belonged to Jerome Baxter, a friend of Stark's going back a decade. Baxter's older brother, Abe, was a colleague of Stark's in the Bureau.

When Stark had reached out to Baxter, speaking in vague generalities about needing a long-overdue break for his family, Baxter had asked no questions.

"Make yourself at home," he had said, and he meant it. He was an accommodating man, yet part of him, too, as the heir of a tobacco fortune passed down through five generations, took great satisfaction in helping others because he relished the power dynamic. There was always a glint of self-satisfaction in his "glad to be in the position to help."

Still, this place offered Sarah some respite from the world, and Francis a place where he could romp around outside and enjoy being just with his parents—when Stark was here.

Stark watched three black horses charge back and forth across a vast verdant pasture. He didn't know whether the horses were stallions or geldings or what breed they were, but these horses were grand in their musculature, athletic and strong and graceful all at once. Their coats shone as if freshly varnished, the morning sunlight sheening off the sleek coats. Francis was asleep in the cabin.

"It's like he has no memory of it," Sarah said. "It's terrifying. It's not like he's blocked it out; it's as if it never happened. As if he has no idea at all. He's going to need help."

"It worries me too. But it might be for the best that he doesn't remember," Stark said.

"I don't see how."

"He's protecting himself from further trauma."

"He *should* be traumatized. What happened is traumatizing." A horse snorted in the pasture, and Sarah glanced up as it trotted off. "It's natural to be traumatized," she said. "I am. You are. I'm afraid he'll wake up and it will hit him hard, all at once. It will break him."

"That won't happen," Stark said.

"You don't know that."

Stark swatted at a deerfly that landed on the back of his hand. "He's still in shock. We'll get him the best help possible, through the Bureau. For both of you."

"For you too." She gave a faint, pained smile. She wanted what was best for him, but her idea of what was best differed from his. "I mean it." She fixed her eyes on his.

Stark wanted to tell her he'd seen worse than what had happened at their house a week ago—much worse. Not just on the job, but when he was Francis's age. He had never told Sarah about Jewel Lake, about what his father had forced him to do.

"We'll be here for him if he does," Stark said.

"I want him to get it out now, not bottle it up like . . ."

"Like me," Stark said.

"That's not what I was going to say." Her voice was barbed. They both knew it was what she was about to say. Fair enough. He agreed. He had bottled up his anger at his old man for decades. Ever since Stark was twelve and the police came to the house to say they had found his mother's body after she'd been missing for weeks. They had arrested the old man. And in that moment, Stark had known that his father had involved him in covering up his crime when he'd taken them out on Jewel Lake in that rowboat. Stark recalled the chilly breeze and the waves rocking the boat as he helped his father hoist two burlap sacks over the edge of the boat. The sacks bulged in ways that made Stark think of malformed gourds. They were heavy and awkward and gave off a stench.

Help me, his father had ordered. *Help me.*

"It will only be worse later," Sarah said, and this time it did sting. She and Stark both knew how bad it could be, how much worse.

"We don't know that," he said.

"We have to sell the house," Sarah said. Her voice wavered, a sadness to it, a resignation to the inevitable; selling the house was the last thing she and Stark had ever imagined doing. They had imagined living there far into their old age. It was home.

Stark watched two horses race across the field, nipping at each other's withers.

"As soon as we can," Sarah said. "We need to put it on the market, find a new house. We can't stay here forever."

"I'll handle it," Stark said.

"It makes me sick," Sarah said. She leaned into his shoulder, and he pulled her close. She wrapped her arm around him, patting his belly as he kissed the top of her head.

Stark was sickened too.

"I'll get things in motion," he said, "as soon as this case wraps up."

Sarah stiffened and withdrew her arm from around him.

"Do what you feel you have to," she said, her voice cold and remote.

She was testing him—unfairly. She and Francis were what were most important to him, and she knew it.

"I can't just quit," he said.

"You could take a leave of absence. No one would fault you." She put her palm to his chest. "No one would feel you were letting them down. Whatever case you're working won't fall apart without you. Some of your colleagues are probably wondering why you *haven't* taken leave. I'm surprised Franklin didn't suggest it, if not insist on it. He probably wonders what's wrong with you."

"Like you wonder?" Stark said.

"I don't wonder," Sarah said. "I know what's wrong. Not *wrong*, but why you're the way you are."

She was referring to his father. And she was right.

"We have money saved, we could both quit outright," she said. "Sell the house. Buy a smaller one farther out, bank the difference. We'd be fine."

"Let's do it," Stark said.

Sarah looked at him. "Don't say that just to mollify me."

He took her hand.

"Let's do it," he said. "Just let me finish this case."

She was about to speak.

"Hear me out," Stark said. "I finish this case and I'm out. *We're* out. I'm seventy percent vested in the pension. Plenty. One thing the Bureau does is take care of its own. I can always work as a consultant. They pay consultants three times as much as they pay their agents, for telling them the same things the agents tell them. You can quit, or work. As you like."

"I'll give you three months," Sarah said, and stood.

She looked down into his eyes.

"There's no telling how long a case will go," Stark said. "It might be three days or three months or—"

"I'm telling you how long I can take," she said. "Three months."

CHAPTER 6

"Brief me," Stark said to Agent King. "Tell me about the suspects and their victims."

Stark, King, and Garnier sat around a circular wooden high-top in the back of the Capitol Diner, a hundred miles west of DC and a hundred north of Richmond, the state capital. Stark didn't know why the diner had the name it did, but the coffee was bearable and the setting private, far removed from the prying eyes at the Hoover Building.

Stark sipped his coffee as he perused the plastic menu.

"First. The text from this S," Agent King said. "She says she knows the three of us are on the case. She's a kook, but how could she possibly know that? It's bizarre."

"It's not bizarre," Garnier said.

King gave a warranted look of confusion. She knew nothing of Garnier or Q or their ability to remote-view. She knew nothing of Stargazer and the program. She needed to be briefed on all these matters as much as Stark needed to be briefed on this case she'd brought to him: that other members of the Six were alleged to have committed murders of scientists.

Until yesterday, Stark had never heard of Agent King. She was just twenty-nine years old, born August 11, 1994. Stark had checked out her background. Born and raised in Biloxi, she had been educated at Hollins and received high honors. She'd maintained a 3.8 GPA in the academy. She was earnest, yet that earnestness was tempered with the maturity and wisdom of an agent ten years her senior. She seemed grounded. Of course, the texts from S appeared bizarre to her.

"Explain it to her," Stark told Garnier.

King looked at Garnier. "Yes," she said, "please explain how someone can text me this—" She took a pair of baby-blue cat-eye glasses from an outer pocket of a black Fjällräven backpack and donned them. She picked up her phone, the colorful beaded bracelets sliding down her wrist, and read aloud: "'It will take more than the three of you to stop me. Soon, just two of you.' And this: 'I know what you're doing. But you don't. You have no idea the havoc you will create if you pursue us. We're doing what needs to be done. You'll see. It's fate. We're a long way from home now. X is the one who's the traitor here.' Who is X?"

"That would be me." Garnier raised a finger.

A waiter ambled over, snatched a pen from the long black hair tucked behind his ear. He wore black jeans and a CAPITOL DINER T-shirt and black boots. Stark imagined him playing lead guitar in a cover band on weekend nights.

"Decided yet?" the waiter said.

Stark ordered two eggs, over easy with bacon.

King glanced at the menu. "I'll have the Capitol omelet and home fries," she said.

"Oatmeal," Garnier said. "And another tea."

With the waiter departed, King asked Garnier, "Why 'X'? Why not your given name?"

"'X' *is* my given name."

King gave Garnier a puzzled look. He didn't bother to explain. Not yet.

"Continue, Agent King," Stark said.

"How can she know there are three of us and that we're investigating her?" King said. "How can she know who I am, or that I'm on this case? I'd only taken the case up that morning, and I'd only just told you about it. Yet she knew in real time? How did she even get my number? She hack my phone? Or have a drone on us?" King asked. "Or what?"

Garnier hesitated as if realizing just how bizarre the notion was that he could view other people and locations with his mind. As if, for the first time, he did not believe the notion himself. "With her mind," he said.

The waiter returned, placed a mug of tea in front of Garnier, and took the other mug away.

King scoffed. "Do not try to make a fool of me," she said.

"I doubt that's possible," Garnier said. He stood. "Look." He pulled down the collar of his shirt in the back and showed King the scar—the same one S had in the photo King had shown him.

King stared at the scar, her dark eyes narrowing. "What is that?"

Garnier faced her. "It's the same scar as S's. In the photo you showed me. I know what we're dealing with because I am one of them. One of six subjects who came from the same place S and Q—these two killers—came from."

"I don't follow," King said.

"I have the same ability that S has. That Q has. To view remote subjects and locations with my mind, or mind's eye—whatever you want to call it."

King sat back in her side of the booth, crossed her arms over her black leather jacket. She glanced at Stark. "Is he serious?"

Stark shrugged. "I wasn't a believer. He's proved me wrong."

The waiter arrived and deposited the breakfasts before the three of them, along with a creamer and a bowl of brown sugar for Garnier's oatmeal.

King sprinkled salt and pepper on her omelet, then doused it with Tabasco sauce. She sipped her coffee and set the mug down, leaving a trace of plum-colored lipstick on the rim.

"What do you mean, you come from the same place as the killers?" King said to Garnier as she tucked a napkin in at her throat before addressing her omelet.

"A program that's part of an organization known as Stargazer," Garnier said.

King remained contemplative. She wasn't a seasoned agent, but she knew the critical importance of listening.

Stark broke his eggs' yolks with the corner of his toast, then mashed the eggs with his fork.

"Stargazer. We were raised in it," Garnier said. "The six of us."

King's expression remained inscrutable.

Garnier told King about his ability to remote-view, how he and five others, among them Q, the Tableau Killer, were raised in what he only recently came to realize was a government program isolated from the rest of the world. None of the six had any recollection of a childhood home or family, even though they were told they'd been voluntarily given up by their families to a place that would help them develop their ability for the greater good.

King's eyes lit with questions.

"And you *believed* that?" she said.

"Kids believe adults," Garnier said. "If an adult says a fat man with a white beard and a red suit travels the world in one night on a flying sled pulled by flying reindeer to bring gifts, you believe it. It just *is*."

Garnier lifted the tea bag from its mug and set it on a napkin. He did not sip his tea. He did not eat his oatmeal.

King was halfway through her omelet, sipping coffee between bites.

"But at some point, kids know better," said King.

"Because older kids tell them the old fat guy is fake. But there were no older kids among us six. It was just us, all the same age. And we were told that we were voluntarily given up by loving parents to use our exceptional gifts to make the world better. We were told we were special and living our destiny to help the world. And we were. We *are*."

"Special?" King said. "Of the six of you, at least two of you are murderers." She pinched her bare earlobe as if checking to see if an earring was there.

"Something went wrong," Garnier said.

"Ya think?" King pushed her empty plate away.

"As with any . . . experiment," Garnier said, "it's—we are—trial and error. Something in Q's and S's minds is broken."

"So, they're not responsible?" King said.

"They're responsible," Garnier said. "But so is Stargazer."

"We don't blame normal parents if their child grows up to become a serial killer," King said. "Why blame this 'program'?"

"We fault the parents if they abused the kid, caused trauma, preyed on them—which is what the program did. I didn't see it until just recently," Garnier said. "I saw my life as normal and my ability as exceptional because I knew nothing else. The program is connected to these murders somehow. There seems to be a purpose behind the murders—a motive, a reason linked to the program—in the killers' own minds, anyway."

King was clearly not having it, not without more interrogation. Stark appreciated it. He knew the doubt and skepticism that needed to be overcome. He knew, too, that King wouldn't really be satisfied without empirical firsthand evidence.

"They sound like your run-of-the-mill killers who think they're smarter than everyone else. In the end, they get caught. Even your genius, the Tableau Killer."

"Q," Garnier said.

"Sounds like a science-fiction moniker to me," King said. She untucked the napkin from her shirtfront and set it down on the table.

"Tell me more about these cases with S. The victims," Stark said to King. The victims often told tales about their killers. The victim was a victim for a reason. The victim told the story about motive and means, about whether the murder was cold-blooded, premeditated, calculated, sloppy, enraged. Stark disliked the term *crime of passion*. *Passion* was reserved for the blush of romance, a cherished pastime, or a labor of love. Not carnage. The term understated the violence and practically excused the perpetrator, as if the passion for the victim that spurred the violence was justified because it was too much for the killer to overcome. The killer just loved her too much. He couldn't bear being without her, so *she deserved it*. She thought she was going to leave *me*?

Almost without exception, it was male-on-female murder.

Passion had nothing to do with it. Hatred, sure. And other

unrestrained dark emotions unleashed with violent results. A tantrum of unhinged violence. But not passion.

"Tell me about the victims first," Stark said. He finished his eggs and was still hungry. "Then we'll cover the perp."

Agent King laid her tablet on the table and opened a file of photos and bios.

She put her glasses back on.

"First is Karl Friede." She brought up a photo of a middle-aged man. It was an amateur shot. His wild black beard was streaked with white at the chops and the tip of his chin. His eyes were narrowed as if squinting into a harsh light. His lopsided smile revealed the yellowed teeth of a man who enjoyed his coffee throughout the day. Not anymore.

"He was a former CEO of Advix, a pharma company. He'd gone into the public sector in his fifties to do research and lecture at MIT."

"About what?"

"Pharmacological therapeutics to help burn victims, and others who have suffered traumatic skin damage, to heal after grafting. He went beyond that too, in vision if not practice."

"How?" Stark said.

"I knew him," Garnier interjected, surprising Stark. Garnier pointed at the photo.

"You knew Friede?" Stark said.

"Not personally. But. I recognize him."

"How?" Stark asked.

The waiter came and topped off Stark's and King's coffees. "Another tea?" he asked Garnier. Garnier shook his head. The waiter cleared away King's and Stark's plates but left Garnier's untouched bowl of oatmeal behind.

"He was a guest lecturer for one of my online MIT classes," Garnier said.

"What was his lecture about?" King said.

"It was eight years ago, or more. He spoke about advances in the treatment of certain blood diseases. I don't recall it standing out in any way. You think his work was somehow part of the motive for his murder?"

"I'm not sure how," King said, "but there may be something there."

"What do we know about him?" Stark said.

"He was fifty-nine years old and a widower. His wife, Marylyn, died in 2017 in a car accident," King said. "Three grown children. As a young boy, he suffered third-degree burns on a third of his body—his entire back and right leg, scarred for life. He was hospitalized for months. This incident guided his life's purpose to create human skin from the DNA of the burn victim herself—as much skin as was needed for grafting back onto the person, and without any scarring. Seamless. He hoped to manipulate the cells themselves so that future burn victims would eventually reproduce their own skin to replace any that was burned or otherwise damaged."

"Commendable," Stark said.

"But not practical, from what I've gleaned," said King. "Skin generation is still decades off. Artificial skin is a hell of a lot likelier than the human body regrowing its own skin where it was burned."

"Tell me about this second victim," Stark said.

"Bonnie Randall. Fifty-two. Never married. No kids. She taught at Stanford. A PhD, she never worked in the private sector."

"What was her field?" Stark said.

A couple entered the diner with two young boys, who looked to be fraternal twins, and were seated at the booth behind Stark. The hostess could have sat them anywhere. It annoyed Stark that she sat them right behind him.

He motioned for King to speak softly.

"T-cell research for diseases," King said, lowering her voice. "Seeking enzyme and DNA and RNA solutions for cures, or, rather, prevention with a focus on cancer—lymphoma and leukemia specifically. She spoke as an authority at symposiums across the globe. Her career was her life. She was educated at Brown University and Yale."

"Find out if she and Friede had any overlapping conferences—were on the same panel or the like," Stark said to King. "Look for the slightest connection between the two. Just being associated with top-tier academic institutions is a connection. It must be a pretty small world.

What about S? Our texter and female perp with the scar."

King leaned back in the booth again and studied Garnier.

"How is it you know a victim and the perp?" she said.

"I didn't *know* Friede," Garnier said. "He gave a single lecture nearly a decade ago. S, I knew."

"How well?" King said.

"Not very. She was nothing like Q, who was a loner and had difficulty restraining himself—his anger, his ambition and vision—who always bucked against authority. When I found out he was the one killing the families, it was a shock, but after thinking about it, I realized he was obsessed, addicted to remote viewing, and would do anything to enhance his ability or at least hang on to it. And he had a hot temper. With S, I am shocked she would even be a suspect. Just because you have a photo of her—"

"She's more than a suspect," said King. "She is *the* suspect."

"I can't see her as violent. She was never a loner, or strange. Never the odd 'quiet type' nor quick to anger."

"No disrespect, but those are pretty clichéd stereotypes. And, after all, you said you don't know her well. So, you weren't really privy to parts of her life, can't really vouch for her either way."

"I didn't interact much with her. True. But every interaction was pleasant. I detected no more than frustration with her. Never anger, not even when she was in pain."

"Pain?" King said. She motioned to the waiter to freshen her coffee. He held up a finger. One moment.

"We all at some point suffered devastating migraines," Garnier said. "Mine just started these past few months—crushing, withering headaches. They put one in a state—a dejected, dark, fuming mood. S's started years ago, as did the others, but she never blamed anyone, the program, for them. She rode them out with no more than modest complaint, even as we were pushed to our limits, and it became clear the migraines and our deteriorating health had to be linked to the extreme trials we endured."

"So, she doesn't seem the type?" King said.

The waiter came over with a pot of coffee. "Still working on the oatmeal?" he said to Garnier, who had yet to put a spoon in it.

"Take it," Garnier said.

"She *isn't* the type," Garnier said to King.

"There isn't a *type*," Stark said.

"Put it this way," Garnier said. "I'm not just shocked by this news that you believe she murdered someone—I don't believe it. Don't believe she *could* do it. It has to be a mistake."

"There's no mistake," King said. "If you recognize the woman I showed you in the photo, you recognize Friede's killer. The photo I showed you is a still from CCTV video showing the murder."

King cued up a video on her tablet.

Stark had thought that the video would be of Friede in his home, or perhaps his MIT office. It wasn't. It was on a walkway. At night. The professor was striding along, looking at his phone, when he turned as if someone had called his name. He nodded and smiled. He seemed pleased to see whoever it was. Perhaps he knew the person. The woman. For it was a woman who now stepped into the frame and drove a knife into the professor's throat, straight into the hollow just above the breastbone. Quick. Decisive. Purposeful.

Yet the professor somehow still managed to grab at his attacker and pull her shirt down enough to expose a scar at the back of her neck. The assailant's face was not fully visible. She was slight and had short black hair, but only the side of her face was visible and only for a frame or two.

"Pause it," Garnier said.

King paused the video.

"Back up a few frames," Garnier said.

One of the boys in the booth behind Stark was peering over at them.

The mother said, "Colton, stop that."

The boy obeyed.

King backed up the video.

Garnier focused on the image with the intensity of a jeweler about to cut a diamond.

"Is that her?" Stark said. "Is it S?"

"I don't know," Garnier said.

"You told me it was her in the photo," Stark said.

"The scar is the same. That's what sold me in the photo. But. Take away the scar, and I'd say maybe, at best. There is something about the side of her face that's not . . . right."

"You can't take the scar away," King said. "The scar is the scar. It's there. It's her."

"It's her," Garnier said in a somber tone that made Stark suspect that he knew this woman better than he could admit, perhaps even to himself.

"Do you know how they might have known each other?" King said. "S and Friede? Did S take classes Friede might have taught or been a guest lecturer at, as with your class?"

"As far as I know, she didn't attend MIT or anywhere else."

"So how do you think she knew Friede?"

"I have no clue," Garnier said.

"Did you ever mention Friede to her?" King said.

"I had no reason to."

"But did you?"

"I didn't. Not to anyone. I had no need. She didn't know of Friede through me. And I haven't really spoken to her or seen her in years."

"Why not?" Stark said.

"The last few years, we were set with different tasks that didn't overlap. I spoke to her in passing, but not to talk to all that much."

"So, she might have changed her positive demeanor?" Stark said.

"It's possible."

"What did you talk about?" King said.

"Not my classes," Garnier said.

"Then what?"

"What anyone talks about. The world."

"It seems you were rather cut off from what most would deem the 'world.' Lived in a hermetic bubble of research and tests and harnessing skills," King said. "No friends. No grade school or high school. No social life. No going on dates or out to bars or to a ball game or a concert."

Stark placed his credit card down on the bill at the edge of the table.

"As I said, I knew her to be a positive person, from the little I saw of her. She found her work helpful, valuable."

"What did her work involve?" King said.

"Intelligence. We all worked in that. She was tasked with locating some of the most dangerous people on earth, some of the most-wanted criminals and fugitives who were a threat to our country and to geopolitical stability."

"Sounds a bit dramatic," King said. "Like whom?"

"I'm not allowed to say," Garnier said.

"Allowed by whom—this program that manipulated and coerced you all, controlling and lying to each of you? The one somehow behind all of this. *That* program?" King said.

"I see your point," said Garnier.

"Who did she help locate? I have top secret clearance. You can tell me."

"Kalik Aswame. A dealer in the depleted uranium needed for certain high-penetration projectiles and tank armor."

King took a note on her tablet.

"Who else?" she said.

"Mikhail Volkov."

King typed in more notes.

"He was involved in an attempted hack into the DOD," Garnier said. "And was responsible for killing several scientists and their families. Q remote-viewed it—the murder of these scientists and their families. It traumatized him, changed him, seeing that."

King glanced at her tablet. "Intriguing. He's traumatized but kills a half dozen families. And this positive, upbeat S—she kills *at least* one scientist."

"She was trying to help, even if she—and all of us—was being manipulated. That's why I don't know how she could ever commit such violence."

"It's common enough," King said.

"Violence like that doesn't seem all that common to me," Garnier said.

"I mean your reaction is common enough. Being unable or unwilling to believe that someone close to you is capable of that kind of violence."

"We weren't close."

"Yet you can vouch for her. Claim you know her at least well enough to say she couldn't do it. Either you knew her well enough to arrive at that conclusion, or you didn't know her well but felt for this woman, this S, enough so that you're letting emotions dictate your response."

"I'm not saying she didn't do it. I'm saying I can't imagine it. There's a difference."

"She *was* manipulated," Stark said. "That's indisputable. You all were. Indoctrinated. Molded. They twisted you around their fingers and kept you in a world of their making—a world of mirrors and shadows and lies. They exploited you in ways you either still can't fathom or are completely oblivious to."

"I'm not oblivious anymore."

"No?" King slid her tablet across the table to Garnier. "Search for the names you just gave me of the fugitives, the most-wanted criminals who S remote-viewed to help capture or assassinate."

Garnier cracked a thumb knuckle and looked at Stark.

"Go on, type in a name," King said.

Garnier typed in a name and hit Search.

Stark sensed what was coming and thought how strange it was that the world, or one's perception of it, could be altered with so simple an act as tapping the Return button on a screen.

Garnier's face confirmed Stark's suspicion.

The waiter returned with Stark's card and set it down. "No rush."

"Type in another name," King said.

Stark watched as Garnier typed with the dispassion of someone in shock.

Garnier pressed Return.

His eyes took on a vacant, dead look.

"Well?" King said.

"So?" Garnier said. "The names don't come up when searched. What does this have to do with me believing that S wouldn't commit such a violent crime?"

"It calls into question *everything* you believe," King said. "Including what you believe about S. The evildoers she claims to have located with her mind—as you see, they don't exist."

"They exist. I saw them," said Garnier. "Saw the footage. So, the program gave us aliases, or the names can't be found in a general online search. They're top secret. That's not a surprise."

"I don't think the program gave S fake names," King said. "I think these men never existed."

"I *saw* the footage," Garnier stressed. "I don't see phantoms."

"They existed. They were real men who died at the hands of this program. But perhaps what the program told you about them was a lie. These men never committed the crimes you were told they committed. They were not at all the people the program made them out to be."

The waiter carried a tray of food out to the family in the booth behind Stark and glanced at the credit card and bill at the edge of Stark's table.

Stark wrote in a substantial tip, signed the receipt, and pocketed his credit card. The tip, he hoped, would buy a few minutes more at the booth.

"Just because the program used aliases doesn't mean—"

"Why are you defending the program?" Stark said.

"I'm not. Why the hell am I being interrogated as if I've done something or I'm hiding something?" Garnier's face was red, his body stiff with resentment.

But he *was* defending the program. It was clear to Stark. Did Garnier not want to admit it, or did he just not realize it?

"I ran the names you just gave me," King said. "In the Bureau's database. None of these names appear. I have access to aliases and real names for those who are a threat to this nation."

"The program has nothing to do with the FBI," Garnier said. "Or the CIA. We're separate."

"You think that men wanted by this program of yours aren't also on the FBI's lists?" King said.

"Maybe the program made up their own aliases so we wouldn't know the real names or official aliases—to protect us, somehow," Garnier said.

"I want dessert!" a boy at the neighboring booth shouted.

"We don't get dessert after breakfast," the father said.

"Or protect itself," Stark said. "For other reasons altogether."

"What if this S was told a fake reason for their needing to be killed?" King said. "Not the real reason the program had for doing it. Because they needed to convince her that killing them was a righteous act to better the world? Would she have believed it?"

Stark recalled what Garnier had posited about Q, that perhaps he'd been manipulated into committing the murders under some false pretense.

"I suppose," Garnier said. "But it's one thing to remote-view intel on a target; it's another to act on the target. None of us ever acted on a target."

"Maybe Q was duped too," Stark said. "We believe he was acting on his own demented notions, down a rabbit hole of his own making. What if he was put up to it without his knowledge? Groomed."

"The families he killed were innocent citizens," Garnier said. "He located them through names he found in documents he stole from Dr. Brady's Arizona home, but he didn't know the names were aliases. He killed innocent families—families that the program had no connection to."

Stark recalled Q telling him about Dr. Brady, who had worked at the program for years before leaving abruptly. Q had tracked the doctor down in the desert, coerced him to tell him the truth, then murdered him and buried him in the desert. According to Q, that is.

But Stark knew that the victim families, by Q's own account and through every investigation Stark had the FBI conduct into their backgrounds, had no connection, however faint. When Q tied them up and demanded they remote-view, none of the victims knew what he was talking about. Q thought the victims were resisting, lying, and it infuriated him. He killed them for no reason.

"Whatever S's motives, it's moot," King said. "Our job is to apprehend her and stop it."

"It's going to be difficult," Stark said. "Whoever sent you those texts, S or another of the Six—he or she can remote-view us. It can't be denied. They might be doing it right now."

"I'll take it at face value that they can do what you claim," King said, "even if it's by some other means we don't understand."

"And just what means would that be?" Garnier said.

King's phone rang. She answered it and stepped away.

She said nothing. Nodded. Looked over her shoulder at Garnier, then at Stark.

"Right," she said.

She ended the call and faced the two men.

"I think we have another one."

CHAPTER 7

The cabin is set back in the Tennessee woods, out of sight of the road. It is a cabin once used by hunters. It's not a family spot, or the setting for a leisurely hike. A low, bellied roof. Board shutters on the inside. A dirt floor. All the shutters but the one in the back of the cabin are shut.

The car is parked around back.

The man is seated in a wooden chair now, wrists bound behind his back to the chair, his ankles too. He faces the cabin door. She stands behind him. Her shadow falls across him.

When he finally stirs, he doesn't struggle. He is a smart man, smart enough to intuit that there is no advantage in wasting energy trying to free himself when he cannot be freed.

His voice cracks. "Where am I?" Randolph says.

"All the poppy-seed cake in the world couldn't get me to divulge that," she says.

"Release me . . . and we'll forget about all this."

"I won't forget," she says.

"Why have you done this? I am no one." He tries to wiggle his ankles without her noticing, but she notices. It's futile for him anyway. Let him wriggle. Let him writhe. Do as he sees fit. He will not escape.

"You help make it all possible."

"Make *what* possible? Nothing that deserves kidnapping me and drugging me, certainly."

"My actions don't absolve you of accountability for your own actions."

"You've made a horrible mistake, a terrible choice."

"Your *choices, your work,* affect mankind."

He scoffs. The nerve. "That's absurd. My work—"

She drags a metal folding chair from where it is propped against the wall. She snaps it open and sits on it, her legs stretched out, bootheels resting on the floor. "Tell me," she says, "what were you doing there?"

"Where?"

"You know where."

"I've been to a lot of places over many decades, and your question is vague."

"You know where."

"Clarify it for me." He works his tongue in his mouth. His mouth and throat are likely quite dry. Good.

"The program," she says. "At Stargazer."

"Never heard of it."

Now she's the one scoffing. She stands and comes to him, lays a hand on his shoulder, and he flinches. "Out west, in the shadow of the Rockies," she says.

"That covers a lot of real estate. I've been all over out here. Vail, Aspen, Denver. Salt Lake, Tahoe, Bozeman. Idaho Falls. Seattle. All over."

"I saw you there. On campus."

"Which campus? Tell me that, and I can tell you if I was there." He flexes and straightens his fingers. They are pale and long, the nails well manicured.

"The campus for the program."

"What program?"

"The program. That's how I know it. Just. At Stargazer."

"I never visited *the program*. I assure you of that. You have me mistaken for someone else."

"You and Dr. Romeau were to give a lecture on genome sequencing."

"Dr. Romeau. Yes, I know him."

"It's coming back to you?" She squeezes his shoulder and sees from this vantage, standing above him, that he is wearing a hairpiece.

"Him I know. I'm not hiding anything or lying. I know nothing about this place called the program."

"It's where you came to speak for Dr. Romeau."

"What you refer to as the program, I know as the Institute for the Advancement of the Human Mind."

If he is lying, he's a master at it. She is tempted to believe him but knows better than to do so without evidence. She comes around to face him, study him.

"You need to tell me what role you play in this," she says as she looks down at him.

"In what?"

"In what the program does—its vision, its mission."

"I don't play any *role* in any of that." His voice cracks, shrill. Perhaps it is simply because of his dry throat, or perhaps he really is this weak. "I give lectures. I sit on panels. I take part in symposiums. I do it for a fee. I do it as a professional, bringing to light my research and my colleagues' advances in our fields. I do not *play a role*. I get paid to deliver information, and then I'm off to the next business or institution that wishes to know the information."

She walks around to face him, squats before him, looks him in the eye. "You do play a role. Whether you know it or not, you do. You must know, of course, that this information you provide for a fee— they don't want it just for the hell of it, for the general enlightenment of humankind. You must know that they use your advances for their own advancement. In that way, you certainly play a role. You can't be so naive as to believe otherwise. Or does the fee you charge help assuage any pesky misgivings?"

She sits again and tilts back in the chair, looks down her nose at him. He is more resolute than she imagined. Or is it stubbornness or perhaps cunning?

"*They?*" he says. "*They* who? You make no sense."

He's agitated, squirming now. Sweat stains the underarms of his shirt.

She sets the chair back down, the front legs stamping hard on the floor. She studies him some more. She believes him. Believes he is ignorant. But ignorance is no excuse, and ignorance does not mean he doesn't know something useful, that *he* isn't useful. He is. Very.

"The men and women you met at the program," she says, "or whatever name you know it by—they've used your studies, your knowledge, your breakthroughs, for their own reprehensible acts."

"Not possible. My studies are in their nascent phases. To implement them in any real way would lead to dire failure. A moral and mortal failure."

"It *has* led to failure," she says. "For many, many years. Do you think they care about failures? Collateral damage?"

"It is not possible."

"You wish that were so."

"In what way could my research be used in a practical sense?"

"They've done something to us. To all of us."

"All of us?"

He is afraid of her now, she sees. Truly afraid. Not because she has him drugged and under her complete control, but because he sees her as unstable. A lunatic. Or he is pretending that's how he sees her, to undermine her.

"The six of us," she said. "The five others and me."

His eyes darken. Fear deepens.

"The intent of my work is to aid humanity," he says.

"*Your* intent," she says, "is not the program's intent. You do know what your research, your findings, could lead to, yes? When you extrapolate out into the future. You do know how it could be misused?"

"That is not my vision. And you'd have to extrapolate decades out into the future."

She slaps him hard across the face.

He cries out in surprise, blinking fast, face going red, not with shame but with rage at the affront. She sees it in his eyes. Yes, rage.

"But you do *know what your research could lead to*," she says.

He doesn't speak.

"Don't you?" she says.

"Of course I know," he says. "I'm not stupid. Any technology can be misused. That is not the fault of the creator."

"No? Not your fault at all? Not the fault of the person who actually brought that ability into being? You are somehow absolved? Detached? They used *your* work to . . . change us. Your work and the work of your predecessors. Are you so blind, so gullible, as to think others would not abuse your work? It happens again and again—'advances' used in ways the inventor swears were never intended. But they had to see the potential for the misuse, the abuses. These are highly intelligent, creative people we are discussing here. They know the repercussions if their innovations are used for ill."

"You can't blame me for—"

"I *can* blame you!" She slaps him again. Harder, so his head turns with the force of the blow. This time, the red outline of her palm appears on his cheek. "I do!"

He grits his teeth.

She paces circles around him, panting. "Who else am I to blame but the one who planted the seed! Who developed the technology to practice this grotesquerie! You gave lectures on it, spelled it out, and demonstrated it step-by-step to total strangers at these symposiums and conventions—for money. Research you do not share with the public. Research you sign an NDA about before giving a lecture on it. Anyone who would pay your exorbitant fees, you imparted dangerous information to them. You didn't do it out of altruism."

"I have a right to make a living."

"You enriched yourself! A hundred thousand dollars for an hour-long lecture. That's not chump change. Your benefactors have deep pockets. Bottomless. Almost as if they're paying you not to think too deeply about what they might be doing with your information."

"There is no *conceivable* way they could implement anything I was working on! They could never put it to real use without harming anyone, or worse." His voice earnest now, desperate, pleading.

"And I am telling you exactly the same thing!" she says. "They *did* implement it anyway. They *did* harm us. They *have* harmed us. And they will continue to harm others. Many others. Millions of others! They don't care if the science is ready or not, safe or not. They can always create more subjects until they work out the kinks!"

"Harm you? Subjects?" he says. "You look fine to me. Normal."

"I am *not* fine! Not normal. Look at me. Look at my neck."

She kneels and turns her back to him, pulls down the collar of her shirt, and runs a finger over the star-shaped scar.

"See that?" she says. "That's because of you! There is something inside me. Something . . . alive. I can feel it. An organism or a parasite or something. Something apart from me, yet of me. It controls me. It might even be why I have my ability."

"*What* ability?" Randolph says. His eyes shine with terror. He no doubt thinks her mad. She is not mad. She is the sane one here. She is the one who sees reality for what it is.

"My ability to remote-view," she says.

He acts as if he doesn't understand, pleading now. "I don't know how it can possibly relate to my field—that scar, or whatever this *ability* you speak of is."

She looks down at him. "I can see things with my mind," she says.

Saying it now feels crazy, makes her feel as unbalanced as he surely thinks her to be. "I'll prove it," she says. She takes hold of his shoulders with both hands. He tries to shrink away, but there is little he can do to evade her grasp. She closes her eyes, and while her fingers dig into his flesh, the rest of her body falls limp. "I see a beach," she says. "Not a tropical setting. Rocky. The Northwest or the Northeast. I'd say Northeast. The East Coast. Maine?"

"Let go of me," he says. "Let go, damn it!"

She grasps him more tightly.

"I see two children dashing toward the edge of waves breaking.

Running down from an old beach house. Both kids blond. An elderly woman waving them in from the porch of the beach house. Another woman with them—their mother. They carry buckets. Colorful plastic pails."

"Get your damned hands off of me!" he yells. "Now!"

But there is nothing he can do. He is at her mercy.

"The woman has short gray hair, very fashionable. And a lime-green one-piece bathing suit with a pink gecko on it."

"Stop!" he demands. "Whatever game you're playing, stop it. Stop it now."

She lets go of him.

"I am not playing a game," she says. "I just proved to you that I have the ability to remote-view."

"You proved nothing. No one can do what you claim," he says. "And whatever trick you do has nothing to do with my work. Nothing. You must have researched the whereabouts of my family before this, to make me think you can just *see things*. It's nonsense."

"Is it?" she says.

She grabs his shoulders again, closes her eyes again, and concentrates.

"The woman with the short gray hair—your wife, I assume now—she's inside the house at a kitchen island, taking a lemon from a bowl and rolling the lemon on the island's granite surface to break the pulp cells down and get more juice from it. Right now. That's what she's doing. Now. She's making fresh lemonade for . . . who? The grandkids."

"More research on your part. She does that every morning—prepares the lemonade for later, for lunch. It's not hard to guess if you've somehow watched her."

"Now she's slicing the lemon and—oh, she's cut herself. Not badly, but enough to draw blood and make her wince and suck at the cut, go to the faucet to rinse it."

She takes his smartphone from her pocket.

"What's the password to open your phone?" she says.

"I'm not telling you."

"Wouldn't you like to hear her voice?"

She watches him ponder this, and knows he'll try to tell his wife where he is or at least what has happened. It's not something he can resist.

He tells her the password.

"And which number is hers?" she says.

"Gloria," he says.

She finds the name and calls the number on her burner phone. She puts the phone on speaker and presses the sharp tip of a syringe to his neck. She shakes her head at him. *Don't think about it.*

The phone on the other end rings. And rings.

Finally, someone answers. A woman.

"Hello?" she says, tentative.

"It's me," he says.

"What are you doing calling from a strange number?" the woman says. "Aren't you supposed to be at a cocktail party?"

"I—"

S pricks his neck with the syringe.

"I . . . just had a quick break from it. You know I hate these things. I thought I'd say hi to the kids."

"You okay? You sound funny."

"Fine," he says. "Tired and busy—can't really talk but just wanted to check in."

"Okay?" she says, perplexed. "Look. I just sliced my finger cutting a lemon, so I can't really talk either."

His face pales. "Is it a bad cut?"

"Stings like the dickens, but I just need to keep rinsing it and get a Band-Aid on it. You sure everything's okay? You sound . . . off."

"I'll let you tend to your finger. Gotta run anyway."

The call ends.

The syringe comes away from his neck.

Randolph stares at her.

"Whatever you're up to," he says, "whatever this is, it has nothing to do with me."

"You understand now. I see it in your face. There is no mistaking it. You know there is no way for me to know she just sliced her finger while cutting a lemon unless I could see it myself."

"No way that I can figure out," he says.

"Keep telling yourself that," she says. "But your own face doesn't even believe you."

"I've nothing to do with it. Whatever *it* is."

"You saw my scar. Something was done to me. To all six of us. And it has everything to do with you and your work—your pioneering vision you claim isn't safe to use on humans and won't be for years. I agree—it isn't safe. They used it anyway. What is it you told them? What, exactly, was your lecture about? And who brought you there to the program? Who were you serving?"

"I wasn't *serving* anyone. You make this out to be a conspiracy, some sort of organized scheme on my end. I was a part of nothing. I do not condone any misuse of my life's work. My work is intended to *help*."

"Then *help* me put an end to those who have appropriated your work for wrongdoing. Help me and I let you go. Give me the names of the people who hired you, those who paid you to visit and to pass along what you know. And I'll let you go."

"You won't."

"I will. I have nothing to lose. I'm dying. I feel it. I know it. I don't have long. I feel as if I am rotting from the inside out, as if my brain, my mind, were made of papier-mâché, absorbing water and slowly disintegrating. I don't have long. And neither does the world. What they did to us is just the start. Help me stop them. Tell me who spearheaded it, who brought you in to speak. Tell me which of them it was."

"I can't."

"Then I will have to go through them all. Each person at the program. Even those who had nothing to do with the Six. One by one. Some might be innocent, but I don't have the time to figure that out on my own. You'll be saving lives, including your own. And your family's."

"My family." His voice pinched with anger.

"I have an associate there now, about to pay them a visit. Before they can enjoy their lemonade."

He tries to lunge from the chair but cannot.

He struggles against his bonds.

She lets him.

He struggles for some time until he tires.

"He's about to knock on their door," she says. "So, tell me who brought you in. I'll give you one minute."

She sets the timer on her phone for sixty seconds and places the phone where he can see it.

Again, she presses the tip of the syringe to his neck.

"I don't deserve this," he says.

"We've got something in common, then," she says.

The timer shows forty-eight seconds.

Forty-seven . . .

Forty-six . . .

"How can I be sure you're telling me the truth about all this?" he says.

"You can't."

"You'll let me go?"

"Yes."

"And you are who you say you are. The things you've told me are true?"

"Yes."

Thirty-four seconds . . .

Thirty-three . . .

Thirty-two . . .

"And if I tell you some names, you'll spare my family? Spare me?"

"Yes."

"Even though I can identify you?"

"Yes."

Twenty-seven seconds . . .

Twenty-six . . .

Twenty-five . . .

"Because you don't have long to live."

"Correct."

Seventeen seconds . . .

Sixteen . . .

Fifteen . . .

"There are two names," he says.

Eleven seconds . . .

Ten . . .

"Tell me," she says.

Nine . . .

He swallows. Blinks.

"Tell me, or the individual will knock on the door to the beach house and introduce himself to your family."

Seven . . .

Six . . .

Five . . .

Four . . .

Three . . .

CHAPTER 8

Romeau smiles as he shuts the laboratory door behind him. "The prodigal son returns, yes?" he says to Q. "And where is your . . . chaperone? He was supposed to be here with you. He brought you in."

"He's not here."

"I see that. Where is he?"

"I don't know," Q says. "He left a while ago and told me to wait here. For you."

"Strange." Dr. Romeau looks around the sparely furnished lab. Looks at the closet door behind Q for a moment, then back to Q.

"Well, I'm sure he'll return to join us," he says finally. He claps his hands together and leans back against a counter. "Why don't we talk until he comes back?"

"I want to see the Man with the White Hair," Q says.

Dr. Romeau lets out a small laugh, then raises an eyebrow. "That's quite the request."

"It's not a request."

"Ah," Dr. Romeau says. "And you feel you can just *demand* such a thing?"

Q places his hands on the back of a stool.

"Go out into the big wide world and return with demands, is that it?" Dr. Romeau says. "Or brought back to us, I should say. You didn't return voluntarily. You've behaved rather poorly out there too. And there's the little matter of your escaping, to begin with."

"I did not escape. I left," Q says. "I was told years ago, by you yourself, that I could leave whenever I liked. The gate was open."

"And you believed this?"

"I didn't yet know that you were a liar. I was told by Dr. Brady as well that I was free to leave anytime. Why should I have doubted it?"

Dr. Romeau paces with his hands behind his back. "Dr. Brady has not been with us for many years. His words from the past are meaningless. But if you had come to us, asked us to open the gate for you, conferred with us about your desire to leave for a while, and why you felt that desire, we might have found a solution for your curiosity about the outside world. Allowed you to leave for the Wilds in a proper fashion, under the right circumstances. Yes." Romeau stops pacing and stares at Q. "But you did not confer with us, with me. You did not seek my counsel and help. Instead, you behaved selfishly. After all we've done for you. All we still do for you. You're lucky they returned you here. You will not be judged or imprisoned here—a far cry from how the outside world would treat you after what you've done. Had you not been returned, you would have rotted in a cell. If not for the generosity and compassion of the Man with the White Hair."

"This is why I wish to see him," Q says. He grips the back of the stool. "I have things I must tell him. Things I now know. But also, I wish to apologize in person and to make amends and show my true regret and remorse for my rash behavior. I also learned things out there that he must know about."

"You can communicate such things to me, and I will pass them along. You cannot just expect to see the Man with the White Hair."

"I can't share these things with you." Q takes his hands off the back of the stool and straightens, cracks his spine. "And I do expect he will want to see what I have to reveal."

"And what is that?"

"Tell him that I know."

"Know *what?*"

"I know what those families were. Tell him I have blood and DNA I want tested."

"Is that so?"

"If the results are not what I think they will be, I'll take whatever punishment is coming. Will welcome it, in fact. That is how certain I am of the results."

"I will speak to him," Romeau says. "In the meantime, make yourself comfortable in your old room."

———

Q steps out into the bright sunshine beneath the big blue sky. He crosses the lawn, sprinkler heads hissing and spitting water to keep the grass green, between the building he has just left and the one ahead of him, a one-story rectangular cinder-block affair—a barracks. His old quarters. He enters the building. The air inside feels dead and trapped. He knows where Garnier is. He always knows. He knows where S is. And V. S and V are joined in this cause, this fight. This war. But the other two—where are they?

Down the hall, he stops at his old doorway and enters his old room. It is as it has always been, spare and small as a jail cell. One twin bed. A stainless-steel bedside table bolted to the concrete floor. No drawer. Just a flat surface on which to put a clock and the books he had to read for his classes. A closet. One small square window in the far wall. Nothing on the white walls. No posters. No prints. No photographs. Blank whiteness. Here, he spent his entire life, not knowing any better until he glimpsed the outside world through the lecturers and scientists and researchers who came and went. He had wanted to learn more from them, but he'd been shut out from these visitors' presentations. Curious and vexed, he had volunteered to set up the chairs in the lecture hall. While he found himself alone, he had gone to a small window in the back of the hall, which from the outside was screened by shrubs, and cracked the window barely a half inch—just enough to let someone hear from outside.

At night he had sneaked out and hidden in the bushes, listening to these men and women who came from faraway places and spoke on strange and wondrous topics in a lexicon he only half understood. At those times, he had taught himself to lip-read. He'd had to strain to hear the presenters clearly, so he focused on their moving lips and, hearing most of what they said, began to discover the rhythms and patterns of the mouth and tongue and lips.

With that ability to read lips, he could remote-view them and know what they were discussing. They had never considered this. His lip-reading was not entirely fluent, making for frequent gaps, but overall, he understood when a guest of honor spoke about the results of tests performed on the Six, or Dr. Romeau and other overseers misled the lecturers.

The program was lying to them.

Q had remote-viewed the presentation of one such lecturer, a Dr. Friede, and when it concluded, Q had slipped from his room and started across the lawn to approach Friede. He came up alongside him. The man was walking at a steady glide, hands clasped loosely behind his back, his head tilted up slightly toward the sky of stars, as if lost in a train of thought.

"We're not what you think we are," Q said.

The man shivered as if startled. He hadn't seen Q come up alongside him. He wore a trim silver suit jacket and pants and a black onyx bolo tie and pointed black boots that reminded Q of a cross between pictures of an early astronaut and TV cowboys he'd seen. It seemed to Q the man had to be someone important, someone with money or power. His face was slender and pale, his mouth small.

"Excuse me?" the man said.

"We're not what you think we are," Q said.

The man frowned. He clearly did not want to be bothered.

"If you don't mind, I'm trying to think," he said. "To concentrate."

"We're not the Institute for the Advancement of the Human Mind," Q said. "We're Stargazer."

"Okay?" the man said, baffled and annoyed. He was sweating now. In the moonlight, Q could see it shimmering at his brow and his upper lip.

"What did they tell you?" Q said.

The man stopped mid-stride. "I don't know who you are or what you're doing here, or what you are going on about, but I have a helicopter to catch." He loosened his tie.

"I live here," Q said. "I work here. I'll probably die here."

The man's frown devolved into a scowl.

"Work here? Die here?" he said. "How old are you?"

"Thirteen."

"What do you mean by all that? You live here with your parents?"

"No. They're—no."

"Where are your parents?"

The violent *thwumpthwumpthwump* of a helicopter, and its flashing, blinking red-and-white lights, invaded the night's quiet dark.

The man resumed walking toward the gate to the campus. He held a palm up to a lock pad, and the gate clicked. Beyond it, the helicopter landed. Dust and grit blew in Q's face, and he ducked from it. When he looked again, the man had stepped through the gate and was on the other side of it. He shut it behind him. The helicopter's blades slowed and stopped as the man hurried toward it.

"Mister!" Q shouted.

"Hey!" a voice shouted behind Q. "Hey!"

Q turned to see Dr. Romeau. He looked angry, but his face relaxed, and he smiled.

"Don't disturb the guests," he said, clapping a hand on Q's shoulder and giving it a squeeze as Q watched the man board the helicopter.

Again, the helicopter's blades violated the quiet of the night with their furious pounding of the air. "What are you doing out here at night anyway?" Dr. Romeau said.

Dust strafed Q's face, forcing him to turn away and spit.

"Let's get you back." Dr. Romeau guided Q by the shoulder as the helicopter took flight.

Q turned to watch the helicopter go.

"Come," Dr. Romeau said. "You're not allowed out here at night. And you've all been instructed time and again to never engage with guests. You know this. They are very busy, very important people. They must not be pestered."

Q suddenly did not trust Dr. Romeau, a man he had always trusted without reservation. Now he was questioning. His mind was humming with questions for the man he had always followed and obeyed. Now he doubted this man.

"Who was he?" Q said.

"A visitor. An esteemed guest."

"The helicopter—it's only for important people."

"Worry about yourself. And doing good work."

"I'm not worried."

"You should be, being out here like this, disregarding basic rules. Besides . . ." He smiled. "You and the others are far more important than that man will *ever* be."

"Then how come I can't go on the helicopter? Can't leave here? Why am I locked in?"

Q had not meant to say these things, had not known he was going to say them. He just blurted them in the moment. It shocked him to hear the words because he realized that these questions had been on his mind, in the back of his mind, for a long time now. Now he regretted saying them. He was afraid but didn't know why he should be. That would come later: knowing why he should be afraid.

Dr. Romeau put his hands on Q's shoulders and looked him in the eye. "You'll get on that helicopter one day. When you're ready. But if you want to, you can leave anytime at all. You don't need my permission. The question I have is, are you ready? Where will you go? What will you do? You're not locked in here. The outside world, with all its terribleness, all its common people—people who are not gifted, who contribute nothing—is locked out. Do you want to leave?"

Dr. Romeau stepped back to the gate and placed his palm on the pad, then pushed the gate open wide.

Beyond the gate was . . . nothing. Darkness. Not a single light in the distance. He knew that there was sage out there, and juniper scrub and grassland for miles, for as far as one could see. And in the distance, jagged mountains.

Where *was* he to go from here?

"Go now, if you like," Dr. Romeau said. "I'll help you pack your bags and some food."

"Now?"

"Tell me where you would like to go, and I'll arrange it personally. Transportation and money enough to get your footing."

Dr. Romeau pushed the gate open hard, so it swung and hit the ten-foot-high fence with a bang.

Q stared at the gap in the chain-link barrier and wondered what was out there, beyond what he could see in the daytime, beyond the mountains in one direction and the dry, dusty plains in the other. He knew there was a world out there. And he knew there were bad people in it. Bad men. His entire young life, he had been told that his purpose on earth was to help the program find these bad men across the world and stop them from harming others. He knew nothing of that world beyond what he'd been told by the Mentors and overseers. He had never read a book for pleasure, though he had spied such books on the shelves of his Mentors, in their offices. He had read only books on math and physics and biology and chemistry and calculus. He had read about wars and enemies, about governments and men and groups that meant the world and the program harm. He had read how badly the natives of this land once treated men who had only come in peace, how those natives had tried to force their pagan ways on the Good Men, had stolen the Good Men's women and children and sold them into slavery, tried to make them give up their god and their native language and customs until the Good Men had no choice but to defend themselves.

He'd been taught everything about the greatness of the Good Men— his people—and of science. He studied and was tested every single day, fifteen hours a day dedicated to the enhancement of his mind and his ability. He and the others were woken at five a.m. and promptly dedicated a half hour to fitness, running three and a half miles around the perimeter of the campus. Then fifteen minutes for breakfast, another fifteen for showering and dressing in daily clothes. At six they began six hours of classes and study and testing of the ability. At noon they ate lunch for fifteen minutes—a sandwich, a salad, and some fruit. Then it was time to really focus on their remote-viewing skills, to harness them and strengthen them, doing drill after drill, testing again and again with objects in nearby rooms, objects on campus, and then things farther afield. Objects and people out in the world. Once a week, their saliva was swabbed, blood was drawn, and they were given injections of vitamins and supplements to help with the rigor and demands. So they were told.

Q opens his desk drawer and takes out a marker and a notepad. He recalls how he and the other five once communicated. It was useful.

He looks at the clock on the nightstand. In another hour it will be time to remote-view V, and V's time to remote-view him.

He writes on the notepad: TAKE THE ENTIRE FAMILY. ALL FOUR OF THEM.

He sits on the edge of his bed and begins to remote-view V.

CHAPTER 9

On the way to Dulles International, King apprised Stark and Garnier of what she had learned on the call.

The murder victim was a Natalie Phyllis, PhD, a researcher at a start-up biotech company, Biovance, which was backed by a private-equity group in Silicon Valley. Her field was biochemistry. King brought up links that were sent to her and read them aloud as Stark drove and Garnier sat in the back seat looking over King's shoulder.

"Biovance creates models of AI and 3-D print robotics to be used in human beings to improve the lives of paraplegics who have suffered a TBI," King said.

"TBI?" Garnier said.

"Traumatic brain injury. And CTE too—the injuries to the brain caused by concussions. It's been in the media on and off the last few years regarding pro football.

"Phyllis was a superstar in her field. Apparently, the injuries are all about electrical signals misfiring or not firing at all, or a blockage that prevents the electrical signals getting from the brain to the nervous and muscular systems. She was brain modeling, trying to replicate what the brain does as far as electrical impulses and 'direction' commands."

Stark accelerated around an SUV that was pulled over in the breakdown lane.

"She was trying to replace the brain with AI?" Stark said.

"Not at all," King said. "Supplement it. Aid it. The mechanical stresses from the brain injury remain."

"It sounds like science fiction," Stark said. He hit his blinker, glanced in the side-view, and glided into the far-left lane.

"Hardly," King said, reading from her tablet. "It's being used today with subjects who choose to take on the inherent risks of experimental trials. It has worked for some individuals, for others it made no difference, and for some few it's been detrimental, even causing death.

"It says here one patient said that with the implant in her brain, she felt 'like a robotic toy doll.' As with people given drugs to calibrate behavior, many patients felt detached from reality and from themselves, as if they were inhabited by someone else. It sounds terrifying, really. Some patients suffered impulsive behavior, hypersexual impulses, dispassion, and violent thoughts. Phyllis's robotics are implanted into the brain to help it send the normal signals. It sounds impossible."

It didn't sound impossible to Stark, but it did sound terrifying. If he thought too long or deeply about the technological future of society and what it meant for Francis as an adult, and for Francis's children and beyond, he could not help but despair. He knew that perhaps all generations of parents held this dread within them, but this was different. The acceleration of technology, AI—all of it felt as though humankind were on the brink of self-destruction.

A car horn startled him. He had let his mind, and the car, drift. He corrected course.

King continued, "But Dr. Phyllis, like the other victims, was a leader in her field. A lauded scholar. She won the Pioneer in Innovation Grant and a Hoyn Fellowship in brain research—two of the most prestigious awards in her field."

Stark had to wonder: Did she discover something that S, if it was

S, or Q didn't want her to discover? Or perhaps Q or S had perceived her as a threat, even if she was not, and she resisted them when they demanded information. Like the families Q had killed.

If it was Q. Or was it S?

Stark pulled off the main highway, the driver of the vehicle he had almost drifted into shaking his head in dismay. Stark didn't fault the man.

———

The body of Dr. Phyllis was seated in a chair facing a window that overlooked a vast plowed field and, beyond it, a gently sloping hill topped by a magnificent old, weathered barn. As Stark stood behind the body and looked out the window, it seemed as if Phyllis were admiring the view.

She was not. She had been dead for two days.

What sat in the chair was not the doctor but the husk that once housed a human being, a mind and spirit. With those two essential aspects gone, the body was no longer the human being.

Its eyelids had been removed so adroitly, with such precision and with an implement so devilishly sharp, it first appeared to Stark that she had died with her eyes wide open, and the lids had never closed.

She was facing forward, her head propped up by a device that cupped the chin and had a rod that cantilevered from her chin to a base that rested against her sternum, arranged so she could not look away from whoever had done this to her.

What had been done to her, besides the cutting away of the eyelids, was not at first apparent.

She was wearing a pale yellow sweater and loose, faded blue jeans. Her feet were bare. Her long red hair, streaked with gray, was drawn back in a ponytail. She wore no makeup. No nail polish. Her dead eyes were opaque and had started to shrivel from desiccation.

Her skin had gone a cadaver gray, purpled and blotched in places, her lips dried and blanched. Her face was bloated with death. And she'd started to have that sour, rancid stench of decomposition and bodily gases escaping her. It would have been a humiliating state to be found in, if she were any longer aware. Which she was not. Fortunately.

Agent King stepped in slow circles around her, thumb pressed to her chin in reflection, brow creased with concentration. She tilted her head to one side, then the other, as if she were in a museum, appreciating from many angles the work of a master sculptor.

Garnier looked on, awaiting his invitation to approach the body and try his skill.

"What happened to her?" King said.

The medical examiner, Rebecca Kage, stood behind them all, outside their ring. She smelled of baby powder. She was a small woman with short gray hair and astute green eyes.

"A tiny, thin, sharp needle, but made of an extremely hard substance, likely titanium," she said, "was inserted into the back of her brain. It would have been nearly instantaneous and likely painless."

"That can kill a person so fast? How?" King said.

"It pierces the brain stem, which shuts down breathing. But it also severs the communication from the brain to the central nervous system, so it cancels out all feeling and pain too. The person doesn't even know it's happening. That is, if it's done with precision, which is very difficult to do. The more likely scenario is that the needle pierces the brain stem but not exactly where it needs to in order to shut down all signals from the brain, or else it is not inserted deep enough. This would cause agonizing pain at the same time it may cause partial paralysis. So, you are in pain yet unable to writhe or try to defend yourself. You know what is happening, what has been done to you, and the pain is meteoric, but you can do nothing about it."

"That's if the person hits the wrong spot?" Stark said.

Kage nodded.

"Or hits the *right* spot, if that's the outcome they want," King said. "Maybe they want the victim to suffer terrible pain and a long, slow death."

"Entirely possible," Kage said.

"How can we know which was the intent?" King said.

"Only one way," Kage said. "Ask the killer."

"What are your thoughts?" Stark said. "Was the intent to make the victim suffer intense pain?"

"As difficult as it is to hit the exact spot, I'd say it's even more unlikely they hit it by accident. If the killer is a layperson and just jabs away, the odds of accidentally driving it into the right spot for instantaneous death are slimmer than if they made the effort to be precise. I believe the killer's intent was to create as much severe, acute pain as possible for as long as possible, while rendering the victim unable to resist yet also conscious and fully aware of what was being done to her. It really is a most exquisitely horrible death."

"What do you make of the eyelids?" Stark asked King.

"I'm speculating the obvious, so I might be entirely wrong. The killer wanted her to see something and not be able to look away," King said.

"See *what* though?" Stark said.

He glanced at Garnier, but Garnier's face was stolid.

"Try your hand at it," he said to Garnier.

Garnier stepped over to stand behind the body and rested his hands on its shoulders. He closed his eyes and went still.

Stark watched him closely.

Garnier's fingers twitched and trembled. Stark could see his eyeballs roving beneath his eyelids, tracking the movement of something.

His hands stopped trembling and seemed to stiffen and lock in place, fingers curling into a taut, frozen claw.

For just a moment, his mouth hung open, slack, as if he were about to drop into a deep sleep or begin to drool. But just as quickly, his mouth snapped shut. He opened his eyes.

"Well?" King said.

"Nothing," Garnier said.

"It looked like something," Stark said.

"A headache," Garnier said.

"You sure?" Stark said.

"Feels like my skull is being crushed," Garnier said.

"I'm not sure what you bring to this anymore," Stark said. "I'm not sure why we should keep you on if you don't bring anything of value."

Garnier's face pinked with embarrassment.

King looked astonished at Stark's bluntness with Garnier in front of everyone. ME Kage busied herself with her tablet.

"Tell me, why should we keep you on?" Stark said.

Stark had no intention of letting him go, even if he would like to. But he needed to press him, to see how much of this was genuine—to see whether Garnier really couldn't remote-view anymore. Just months ago, when Garnier first came on board, Stark had outright dismissed his so-called ability. Now Stark had to wonder whether Garnier was remote-viewing and keeping what he saw to himself, for reasons unknown.

"The last few times, you've come up with nothing," Stark said. "Except a headache, exhaustion, confusion, complaints. We've got nothing from you. So, I respectfully ask, what is the point of our keeping you on payroll?"

"Perhaps there is no point," Garnier said. "I told you from the outset, I am no crystal ball. My ability doesn't turn on and off with the flip of a switch. I'd rather not be doing this, honestly. I'd rather be doing *anything* but this. It feels as if my head is in a vise. It makes me ill. Not just my attempts at viewing but all of this. The violence. The deception. The machinations. The lies and politics. All of it. I'm trying to use what meager skill I have to help, for something positive, and if I cannot do that to your liking, then yes, let me go. I'll welcome it. I've no idea where I will go from here, but I won't have to be immersed in having to see the worst depravity human beings unleash on one another. I won't be a party to *this*." He nodded at the victim's corpse, then stood in front of the window, his back to Stark, and looked out across the furrowed earth.

Stark surveyed the scene out the window. It was a pastoral view of a hillside. A stacked-stone wall bordered the field, edged along woods of maple and oak and an understory of thickets. Once, this had all been fields. It had looked like much of Ireland or Scotland, bare of trees and chopped up into tracts by rock walls meant to keep in the sheep that roamed the hills. Near the top of the hill stood the enormous barn.

Impressive though it was in size, it did not seem sound. The entire structure leaned west and looked as if the next strong gust might push it over in a pile of lumber and nails. Its corrugated-metal roof was rusted and buckled. A wayward flap of it had come loose and hung over the eave, exposing the skeletal rafters.

There was nothing to see out there.

Garnier made a sound as if he were clearing his throat, only deeper, down in his chest. A grunt.

He pushed open the French doors that led out to the backyard, stepped outside, and stared up the hill at the barn. The wind blew, and a flock of starlings swept across, low over the field, moving in concert as if each were tethered to the next.

Stark watched Garnier.

"What's he doing?" King said.

"Your guess is as good as mine," Stark said.

"My guess is there's something drawing him to it."

Stark said nothing.

Garnier continued to stare at the barn.

After several minutes, Garnier started to plod up the hill, his head down.

Pausing halfway up the slope, hands on his knees, he looked up as if to make certain his destination was still there.

He started up again.

On the side of the barn was a crooked door facing the house. Garnier was headed for it. It seemed he intended to go inside the barn.

But as he crested the hill just in front of the barn, he didn't go in. Instead, with his hands tucked in the pockets of his loose trousers, he turned around and looked back down at the house. Now he studied the house with as much focus as he'd had looking up at the barn.

"He's an odd one," King said.

"You're the preacher; I'm the choir," Stark said.

Garnier seemed to be looking down the hill into the window where Stark and King stood. Seemed to be watching them. But there was no way he could see them. The angle of the sun on the glass was likely turning the window into a mirror.

Garnier walked around the west side of the barn and disappeared behind it. Stark waited for him to reappear.

After several minutes without a sign of Garnier, Stark said to King, "Come on."

The two of them climbed the hill. It was steeper than it looked from the house.

The sun glared down—hot already for not even ten in the morning.

The ground was hard, and the sloping field, which from a distance looked like a uniform mat of swaying grasses, was rutted and rocky and infested with nettles and goldenrod.

At the top of the hill, in the shadow of the barn, Stark looked back at the house. King stood beside him, doing the same. Stark mopped his brow with his shirtsleeve.

There was nothing out of the ordinary to see here. A patio with tall grass coming up through the cracks between the stones. The back of the house was ordinary—windows and French doors, shutters and gutters and downspouts. Nothing of note.

Stark walked around the back of the barn. Here the sun shone even brighter. The field continued for a few hundred more feet, and beyond it, beyond the cliff, the Atlantic glimmered like molten silver.

A stiff wind gusted, swaying the grasses.

Garnier must have been inside the barn. Its doors were open, parted a few feet on the old, rusted track.

Stark went inside. It took a moment for his eyes to adjust to the dimness, even with the slanted bars of sunlight slicing between the barn-board siding. Dust motes corkscrewed in the air.

"Garnier," he said.

"Here," said a voice in the gloom. It was Garnier, though it didn't quite sound like him. The voice had a quavering tone.

King remained outside the barn and was wandering toward the edge of the sea cliff.

"Look," Garnier said.

Stark could just make out his form in the shadows.

He crouched. Bent over. Looked at something on the dirt floor of the barn.

Stark walked over. "What is it?" he said.

"Boot tracks." Garnier stood up and nodded down at the dirt.

Boot tracks. Yes, he was right about that.

The boot tracks were odd because they faced the barn wall, the toes almost touching the base of the wall. Whoever stood here had been looking out between the slats of the barn wall.

"Someone was watching the house," Stark said.

"And look." Garnier pointed at the dirt. More tracks. Whoever made them had walked along the edge of the wall to the small door that opened onto the field, overlooking the house.

In the dirt by the door were scuff marks, where the door had been opened into the barn.

Garnier opened the door, as if to show Stark what had created the scuff marks.

In the grass just outside the door were impressions made by the same boots. Whoever had stood here had done so for some time, and in recent days.

"Whoever stood here wanted to be seen by her, the victim," Garnier said.

"Maybe," Stark said. "We can't know for sure if the individual stood here while the victim was still alive."

Garnier considered this. "For that matter, why stand here at all?" he said. "If the person wanted to be seen, why not stand just outside the window where the doctor was seated? Or just stand right there in the same room? Dr. Phyllis was tied to the chair. She couldn't move to hurt the person. So why stand up here?"

Why indeed? Stark pondered. The boot tracks were those of a man, no doubt. A big man. A heavy man.

"The eyelids," Garnier said. "That was so she couldn't look away from the man standing up here. They wanted her to know that he was up here. They wanted her to know who was behind what was being done to her."

"Agent Stark." Agent King stood at the entrance of the sliding barn doors, her shadow long on the dirt before her. "Agent Stark, I need you to see something."

Stark and Garnier left the barn to come back outside into the bright, assailing sun.

"This way, sir," King said. She walked toward the edge of the cliff at a swift, determined gait, pushing through the sea of grasses and nettles undeterred.

Stark stood at the precipice of the cliff, flanked on either side by King and Garnier.

"There, sir," King said. She pointed down toward the narrow strip of rocky beach, where the body of a man lay broken. A big man. A heavy man.

——

It took nearly a half hour to pick their way down the cliff, following a mostly disused footpath along the top until it came to a more modest descent that switchbacked several times before bringing them down to the beach. It was not really a beach—the seashore, yes, but there was no sand to speak of, and many of the rocks seen from above were boulders the size of a bulldozer, jagged and sharp.

It took another half hour to scramble around and over the least precarious of the boulders and outcroppings until they finally reached the corpse.

Seagulls flew up from the rocks upon their approach, squawking and crying in their plaintive, demanding manner.

The corpse had been at the bottom of the cliff for a couple of days—since Phyllis was killed, Stark gathered.

It was in rough shape. Whoever this man was, he had fallen from the cliff. Whether he was dead before he fell, or the fall had killed him, was for Kage's autopsy to determine. But whether he was dead or alive when he hit, gravity and the rocks had done massive damage. It was an ignoble end. His skull was broken open like a dropped pumpkin, fractured arms and legs akimbo at odd angles. Hermit crabs scuttled over the body—so many crabs, in fact, it looked at first, from a distance, as if the body were encrusted with crawling barnacles.

But as Stark approached, many of the crabs retreated beneath the rocks, giving the illusion that the body was moving.

Stark and King and Garnier stood around the body. The boulders here were dry, above even the highest tide, though the waves crashing on the rocks just below sent up a fine mist that moistened Stark's face.

He looked back up at the cliff. It was a long fall, at least a hundred feet.

Blood coated the rocks around the body.

Had he died before his fall? Had he *been killed* before his fall? Pushed? Did he jump? Fall by mistake? These were the scenarios that needed to be eliminated until one possibility remained.

The man lay face down on the rocks, which was a blessing really. Stark didn't care to see the damage done to the face. The man was tall; even with his body badly broken, one could tell. And big. Broad. He wore Greenbrier pants and a black turtleneck, like a seaman, and on his feet were a pair of chunky black work boots. Stark had no doubt that the prints of this man's boots would match those in the dirt of the barn floor and in the grass outside the barn. This was the man who had stood out there during the torture and killing of Dr. Phyllis. Stark had thought the man was there on purpose, had been a part of the killing in some way, made to stand up on the hill by the barn so Phyllis could see him and know who was behind her demise.

Or perhaps that was not it at all. Perhaps this man was a local who had witnessed the crime from up here on the hill and been discovered in the act and had to be taken care of, removed from the equation.

Despite the outdoorsy clothing, this wasn't someone who worked on the land or labored physically in any way. His hands were pale and smooth, his fingernails trimmed and buffed.

The sound of the water on the rocks jarred a memory loose in Stark—the second time it had come to him in recent weeks. A memory he hadn't dredged up in twenty years.

He and his father, in the rowboat on Jewel Lake. Waves splashed over the side, and Stark, just eight years old, worried that he and his father might drown.

Help me, his father demanded. *Help me.*

Stark looked at the man dashed on the rocks and tried not to think about the damage a hammer could do to a human skull. He thought about how, when the police had come to their door and asked if his father knew anything about burlap bags snagged by a fisherman in Jewel Lake, his father had said no. And then how furious he had become when his young, naive son had blurted, *I bet those are the ones we dumped from the rowboat.*

Quiet! his father had shouted. *The boy doesn't know what he's saying.*

Stark recalled the day leading to his mother's disappearance. That afternoon, his father had been nailing decking on the back porch as seven-year-old Stark looked on, a plastic hammer in his hand. His father struck each nail with precision, never leaving a hammer mark in the decking.

Later, his parents visited neighbors down the block to swim in their pool. Stark was left alone. He recalled his mother putting Band-Aids on the backs of her heels before she left. She had treated herself to her first new pair of sandals in years, but they needed to be broken in.

"Treating yourself an awful lot lately," Stark's father had said.

With his parents gone, Stark took his father's hammer and tried to pound nails into the deck. In the early evening, he knelt over yet another bent nail, furiously trying to extract it, clawing at it and the decking with the hammer, when his old man came from behind and kicked him in the tailbone, sending him sprawling.

The old man picked up the hammer and stared down at Stark. "Where's Mom?" Stark had asked. His father stalked away.

Stark's mother had sneaked into Stark's bedroom late that night to find him awake, curled up and sweating in his sheets. She had lain beside him, wrapped him under her arm, resting his head on her chest. There was a musky, sweaty odor about her. She stroked Stark's hair and kissed the top of his head as he whimpered. "Forgive me," she said. She left and returned with an ointment and rubbed the cool cream into Stark's aching backside where the old man had kicked him, until Stark fell asleep to her nursing hands and whispered apologies. "Forgive me. Forgive me."

The next day, she vanished.

"She's run off," his father had said. "Finally left us. Her only child. Just . . . left you."

For months, Stark had lived with this as the truth, until the police came to the house and asked his father if he knew anything about two burlap sacks that a fisherman had snagged at the bottom of Jewel Lake.

A wave crashed, jolting him back to the present.

He imagined now that the first law enforcement here on this site had searched the entire property, the barn itself. Evidently, no one had thought to go to the cliff and look down.

"What made you look down?" Stark said to King.

"The seagulls. They were making more of a racket than anything I'd ever heard. I looked down and saw dozens flying in a circle and landing and squabbling with each other over him." She looked at the body. "I couldn't make out what it was at first."

Stark took out his phone and made a call. "I'm at the base of the cliff behind the barn," he said. "We need Kage and forensics down here, and more forensics in the barn."

————

The forensics team of three taped off the area and had Stark and King and Garnier keep back while they worked their way toward the victim from a distance.

The man had no ID. Whether he came here without it, or someone took his ID from him, or he lost it in the fall, Stark could not know. Perhaps it would turn up in a more rigorous search among the rocks, using canines.

Who was he? Not just his name, but who? What kind of life had he led? Why was he here? What had he seen? Who had seen him? He was a big man and, Stark surmised, not one to be easily overcome physically.

When the forensics team was done, Agent Kage came over to Stark. "What's it looking like?" Stark said.

Kage popped a mint in her mouth. "No way to tell until an autopsy shows if he suffered injuries or poisoning or some other means of death before the fall. Even then it might be hard to determine whether he ended up here of his own accord or not. The team up there"—she glanced to the top of the cliff—"reported they found nothing to indicate a struggle or a prefall injury. No blood. No disturbed grass or brush or rocks. If he wasn't dead before his fall, I can tell you that's a long ways up and a long time to have to think about what's going to happen to you. It would take almost two and a half seconds. That's an eternity."

Stark looked up at the top of the cliff.

One thousand one.

One thousand two.

One thou—

It was a long time to know what was coming.

"Sometimes a person will go into cardiac arrest in such instances," Kage said. "The fear is so profound and acute, it fires a jolt of adrenaline that the heart cannot bear. No sign of any ID up there? A wallet? Any sort of personal belonging that could help us?"

"Not yet," Stark said.

Was it better to know that your death was coming, or to never know what hit you?

To die in your sleep as Stark's friend had died at the age of fifty-two from an aneurism. Fall asleep. Never wake up. You never knew you were dying or about to die. You exist; then you do not exist. And when you no longer exist, you don't know it.

Stark thought about such a long fall from the cliff. It would give him time to conjure the faces of Sarah and Francis, remember one golden moment in his life with them, and whisper his love for them, keep them in his heart and mind as the earth came screaming up at him. He did not think it would be so bad. Knowing. He believed he would prefer it.

He wondered if his mother had known what was coming. Stark had never dared ask his father if he at least spared Stark's mother from knowing that her death was coming at her husband's hands. A man she had been in love with, once. A man who had loved her. Stark had seen it. His father had loved her and was not always so consumed by jealousy and suspicion. He had not always had the need to control his wife's behavior, know her every move, and monitor each penny she spent. The old man no doubt would claim to this day that he still loved her and loved his son. Little Lukie. Which made who he was and what he had done all the ghastlier. Stark hoped, twenty years later, that his mother had been killed without knowing who her killer was, without that final added heartbreak. Being murdered by your husband was not the same as falling from a cliff. The cliff could not be faulted.

The only act more horrible to Stark was the fact that the justice system had just recently seen fit to grant his father parole. He was a free man. He was out in public, and he had made a surprise visit to Stark, parking across from his house the night after Q's attack.

An agent scrambled over the barnacled and mussel-encrusted rocks to address Stark.

"No one's been reported missing in the greater region that fits the man's description," he said. "And there was no vehicle found anywhere nearby that the man might have used.

"Helicopters flew the area in a twenty-square-mile sweep and found nothing. This likely means either his vehicle was driven away by someone else after the fact, or someone dropped him off—someone who hadn't reported the man missing, because they couldn't afford to report it."

Stark's phone rang.

The number gave him pause. He answered as he turned his back to Garnier and King and stepped away.

"When?" Stark said. "How?"

As he listened, he turned to watch King, whose back was to him now. She pressed a palm to the side of her head, as if she were trying to compress a wound and keep herself from bleeding.

Stark said, "Okay. Let me know."

The call ended, and Stark stood there processing what he had just been told.

"What?" Garnier said.

"It's Franklin," Stark said.

"What did he want?"

"Nothing. He's dead."

CHAPTER 10

Q holds up the notepad for V to read as the two remote-view each other at their appointed time. Q watches V park the car at the end of the long gravel driveway to the Maine beach house.

V gives an emphatic nod that he has remote-viewed the note.

Q tears up the piece of notepaper and tosses it in the trash.

The door to Q's old bedroom opens. It is Dr. Romeau.

"Follow me," he says.

Q follows him to the lecture hall.

When he and Romeau enter, the doctor averts his eyes from the small stage where a lectern stands.

"He'll arrive shortly," Dr. Romeau says as he exits.

And soon the Man with the White Hair does arrive, from behind a curtain on the stage.

———

"Come," the Man with the White Hair says. "Sit." He gestures to the front row of seats.

Q sits.

The Man with the White Hair is much smaller than Q imagined. Q has always imagined a big man, tall and powerful. He is not merely short; he is small. He is proportioned, but everything about him is diminutive, as if he stopped growing at thirteen years.

The Man with the White Hair takes position behind the lectern, perched on a step stool. He fiddles with his red bow tie and fusses with the red handkerchief peeking out from the breast pocket of his blazer.

He taps the microphone in front of him and lowers it in its stand so that it is in front of his tiny mouth.

There is no need for the microphone. He is only a dozen feet away from where Q sits, and the acoustics in the empty space make every little sound resonate.

"You are back from the Wilds," the Man with the White Hair says.

The Wilds? Was that what he called the outside world? The real world?

Q says nothing. Does nothing.

He no longer fears the Man with the White Hair. Nor does he respect him. He always feared and respected him because he never saw him. The man was the myth, but no longer.

Here he is, the Man with the White Hair, the person Q has heard of his entire life, someone he began to think of as a metaphor created by those high up in the program to instill a healthy fear and awe in the Six. A man spoken of with the reverence held for a deity, the Omnipotent One, who could see and feel all others from afar. The Overseer. These were other monikers used to describe him. Now Q is here with him, face-to-face.

Q does not know his name or if he even has a name.

He doesn't care.

The Man with the White Hair is, as far as Q can tell, just a man. An old, small man with a paunch, and white hair gone yellow as antique piano keys. The same hair sprouts from his ears.

He is a man out of myth, but nothing mythical; he is a side character, one who lives in a straw house or under a bridge.

The microphone squeals and squeaks. The Man with the White Hair scrunches up his face, purses his lips, and wrinkles his nose as if he has caught an unpleasant odor. "Why did you act out in this manner?" he says. "Why do you make demands? Why did you flee? What led to this behavior?"

"You know," Q says.

"I assure you, I do not."

Q ponders. The Man with the White Hair knows. He has to know. He is merely trying to coax it out of Q—an admission. Have Q confess aloud what the Man with the White Hair already knows.

"I believe you do," Q says. "And you ask me now just to hear it from me, as a form of humiliation. I won't be humiliated."

"Enough. You came to apologize. So, apologize. Now."

"I've done nothing that deserves my apology."

"No one speaks to me this way!" The Man with the White Hair clenches the microphone. "No one speaks with such a tenor of defiance and belligerence. No one. Apologize."

"The truth," Q says. "Isn't that what we were taught? The truth is the bedrock of all our behavior here. Even when the truth might sting—might hurt us or wound us or humiliate us—we speak it anyway because it is the only way to advance. It can only better us. Isn't that your mantra? I ask now, truthfully. Do you not know why I did what I did?"

"This is insubordination." His face reddens with fury, and his fingers clutch the sides of the lectern as if he might lift it above his head and slam it down.

"I am not your subordinate," Q says. His blood is hot in his veins. His temples throb, but not with pain. Even now, after what he did to those families in the name of what was right—even now, seeing that the Man with the White Hair is just another man with no power over him—he feels a frisson of fear run through him.

"You shall not speak to me this way!" the Man with the White Hair shouts. His voice reverberates all around the hall, surrounding Q.

Q stands.

"Sit!" the Man with the White Hair demands. "Be seated!"

"I won't sit," Q says. "You know why I left. You know why I did what I did. That they had what I needed."

"What did they have that you needed so badly?"

"Proof," Q says. "Proof."

"You had no right to do it, no authority to act alone, to upset our existence."

"I needed what they had. Here. Here it is."

Q reaches into his pockets and produces the glass vials. "I did the dirty work. You. You need to see that the lab work is done, and I will be there the entire time to witness it all."

"What did you do?"

"What had to be done."

"You could have done it another way. Collected samples by less violent means."

"No. I needed to destroy them, the *families*—"

"If you know you are right, you won't need samples tested."

"I need them tested to show others, to have empirical proof and not just my word. You will see that the lab work gets done. Compare the samples to one another and to mine. And"—Q stares him in the eye—"to yours."

"Never! I will not be tested like—"

"Like *me*? You will. I will see to it. If the results don't show what I think they will, I am all yours to put to work as you see fit, in any way you like. Or to put down. Either way, I'll never leave again."

"And if they do show what you think they will show?"

"You don't want to know what I will do. You didn't bring me back. I am here because I set it in motion. My return. I manipulated Garnier and Stark into believing this is where I would least like to be, knowing you'd never have taken me back simply as a prodigal son. I had to let it be you who brought me back. I had to satisfy your ego, your narcissism. So, I plotted to have myself traded back to you, and come back where I can't be found, to a place unknown to the outside world—the place I need to be, for now."

"You owe us everything," the Man with the White Hair says. "You owe us your very life."

Q picks at a thumbnail.

"Killing those innocent families for no reason was an abomination," the Man with the White Hair says.

"I had my reasons."

"Explain!"

"I know who these families really are. *What* they are."

"Which is?" the Man with the White Hair says. He leaves the podium and comes down the stairs to stand in front of Q. Look down on him.

"They are not what I told the FBI they were," Q says. "You know this."

"Do I?"

Q likes this man less and less with his answers that are questions, trying to sound wise when he is arrogant and vague. "I knew the names on the sheets I got from Dr. Brady were genuine. I know," Q says. "So, are you going to test the samples I have, or not?"

The Man with the White Hair closes his eyes as if experiencing a sublime revelation.

Q sinks the syringe deep in that skinny neck. He watches with satisfaction as the Man with the White Hair goes rigid, eyes blinking fast, then going wide and unblinking.

Q drags him to the corner of the room and lays him down on the floor. Pulls a drape from the window and covers him with it. As he does, the Man with the White Hair's eyes go wider with disbelief and utter confusion. Does he truly not understand why any of this is happening? No matter, he will understand soon enough.

CHAPTER 11

The elderly woman stood at the kitchen island, stirring sugar and water on the stove to make simple syrup for the grandkids' homemade lemonade. Hearing the knock at the front door of the beach house, she looked up.

It was friendly, light—a quick, jaunty *rap rap rap.*

It was the type of rap she might expect from someone whistling a chipper tune and holding a bouquet of wildflowers. It was that sort of knock.

The woman hesitated as her simple syrup simmered on the stovetop. If she left it for more than a minute or two, it would be ruined. If she took it off the heat, it would be ruined. She turned the stovetop down as low as it would go and wiped her hands on a dish towel.

The rap came again.

The woman looked out the window at her daughter and her twin granddaughters. The three were bent over at the ocean's edge, picking up seashells, inspecting them, and placing them in colorful plastic buckets.

The woman gave the simple syrup a last quick stir and crossed the room to answer the door.

The pad of her thumb stung where she had cut it slicing a lemon, and she sucked on it as she approached the door. She had read somewhere recently, in *The New Yorker*, or perhaps it was *Harper's*—somewhere, anyway—that sucking on a wound was a part of our evolution, that the enzymes in one's saliva helped a wound heal faster. She wondered if that was true.

Just as the rapping resumed, she opened the front door.

The man who stood there smiled.

It was an awful smile, and the woman knew in a beat of her heart that opening the door had been a grave mistake.

His smile was all wrong, crooked and cruel, and his eyes were too wide, with a manic shine to them. Before she could shut the door on him, he had somehow stepped inside, quick as a cat.

He must have sensed what she was about to do next because he put a finger to his pale, thin lips and said, "*Shhhhh.*" Then he ran a finger across his throat in a cutting motion.

She lunged for the patio door. She wanted to race out past the dunes and across the beach to the water, where two generations of herself played, oblivious to what was unfolding here.

She wasn't even able to get her back to the man when she felt a sharp jab in her neck, the sting of a hornet. She felt her consciousness melt away like a sandcastle at the edge of the lapping waves.

CHAPTER 12

Wallace Germaine and Vivian Sadler. S doesn't know the names.

She thought she would know the names Randolph gave her. She thought the names would confirm her theory. They don't. She has no idea who this Germaine and Sadler are.

She contemplates the situation. Was this a ploy by Randolph, giving S two erroneous names to buy his freedom only for her to find a dead end?

"I've never heard of either of them," she says.

"Those are their names," Randolph says. "The names I was given. I have the letters, the invitations with their names on them, when they first reached out to solicit my appearance."

"They sent invites?" she says. "In the mail?"

"Email. I printed them."

"What about the emails themselves? Aren't they on your phone?"

"Not anymore. It was years ago. I keep hard copies. It's easier for me, filing them that way. I'm not a young man versed in all that, as is evident."

It is possible she didn't know everyone at the program. In fact, it is highly probable. Still, she thought she would recognize the names.

"I'll look into it," she says.

"You're not letting me go?"

"Not yet."

"You said you would."

"I will. Just not until I verify the names. I have to make sure you're not lying."

"I'm not. I swear."

"Then you have nothing to worry about."

"What if something happens to you while you're gone? You get caught or get in a car wreck, or something happens, and you can't get back here to untie me?"

"Try not to think of such scenarios. It won't help matters. Drink some water and eat this." She holds a bottle of water to his lips and tilts it, spilling some. He drinks all of it, pausing for a breath just once. She offers him a cold chicken sandwich she bought at a convenience store when she stopped for gas.

She feeds him. He eats fast, grimacing after each bite. It doesn't look like the most appetizing sandwich.

When he is finished, she gags him again.

"Now," she says, crouching beside him. "Tell me, where can I find these invitations?"

"Filed away. In my home. But I can't let you enter my home."

"Then I can't let you leave."

"My home is five hundred miles from here."

"I have a car. Give me the keys to your house."

"I don't have a key. It's a code."

"Give me the address. And the code."

He hesitates.

"The sooner I confirm, the sooner we get this done."

He gives her the address and the code for the front-door lock.

"If either of these is incorrect, I'll never come back."

"They're not incorrect. You'll need the alarm code too," he says.

Maybe he is on the up-and-up, S thinks. She could easily have entered his home and triggered the alarm, bringing the police.

With the code to the alarm system in hand, she departs for Randolph's home, five hundred miles away.

CHAPTER 13

Franklin's body lay on the plush white carpet of his living room. The furniture was of chrome and steel and glass, the couch streamlined and low.

Franklin was on his stomach, his cheek pressed to the immaculate white carpet, as if looking for keys or a wallet beneath the couch.

His hands were at either side of his face, palms down as if, any second now, he might push up off the floor and walk away after finding whatever it was he had lost.

His gray sweatpants had an athletic fit. His feet were bare, the soles pink.

Stark felt embarrassed for his former superior.

An ME, Blake Hansen, stood beside Stark. He had worked with her on prior cases. She was no-nonsense, focused, and diligent. Her auburn hair was swept back in a tight ponytail, a few white strays catching the light.

There was no sign of violence. No chair amiss. Magazines—*Architectural Digest*, *Smithsonian*, and *Virginia*—were stacked neatly on the glass coffee table.

"I want to show you something," Hansen said, and knelt beside

Franklin's body. She looked up at Stark. "Here." She cradled Franklin's head gently in her gloved hands and turned it slightly. There was blood there, on the side of his face that had been against the carpet. Part of his cheek was still stuck to the carpet with it.

"He was struck," Stark said.

"We'll determine that for certain later. For now, I'd say he wasn't struck but that *he struck* something. The corner of this coffee table. I believe he fell and struck the side of his head on the hard, sharp corner." She touched the corner of the coffee table. "It's been processed for DNA—hair, blood, skin," she said. "The wound is in proportion to the corner."

"Fell or was pushed," Stark said.

"I can't count that out, but there is no sign of a struggle."

"Things can be tidied up, put back in place," Stark said.

"True."

"Fell how?" King said. "How does a person just . . . fall?" She looked around the room.

Hansen said, "We trip over the edge of a carpet or over our own selves. It happens. Especially if we're distracted or tired."

Stark was having trouble with it. Within days after Franklin retires—extracts himself from the FBI, from any attachment to Q and the program—he trips and brains himself on the coffee table. It was too fantastic. Improbable. Stark's mind could not let it go.

It all reminded him of a cat he had as a child. Mr. Whipple was primarily an outdoor cat. He came and went as he liked, following his own feline urges. He was more of a freeloader boarder than any kind of pet. He would meow to be let out at night, and if he wasn't let out straightaway, he'd mewl and caterwaul until Stark's father muttered, "That thing—somebody, let it out."

The cat would nap most of the day in the house. Wake to eat, perhaps get an ear scratched by Lukas or his mother, then go back to napping until evening, when he got restless to be let out to hunt all night. From time to time, he'd return with burdocks in his fur or scratches on his face.

Then one morning, Stark had found Mr. Whipple dead in their basement. He'd gone down to the cellar to get a pack of frozen peas from the chest freezer for his mother and found the cat in the corner. At first he thought Mr. Whipple was just sleeping. But he quickly understood this was not the case. The cat was lying on its side with its front and rear legs stretched out—a pose it sometimes took while napping in a patch of sun coming through a window. But there was something odd about it. Something too still. Unnatural. For one thing, there was no sun to stretch out in down in that dark corner of the basement.

Stark had knelt beside the cat. It was clear the animal was dead, even before he rested a hand on it and felt how cold and stiff it was.

Even up close, Mr. Whipple had not appeared injured. He'd looked asleep.

But when Stark turned the cat over, its face was bloody and flat, a misshapen grotesquerie. To this day, Stark had no idea what had happened to his cat, whether it had been struck by a car during the night or attacked by another animal or abused by a human. It also remained a mystery how it had managed to find its way into the basement as badly injured as it was. His father had told Stark that it had probably been hit by a car and had dragged itself home to die where it felt safe.

Stark doubted this. The cat was so gravely injured, he didn't see how it could have gotten home on its own. But how else could it get there? Someone would have had to bring it into the cellar dead. Unless somehow an animal—a raccoon perhaps, or a fisher cat—had gotten into the basement and killed the cat there.

Sometimes we never get answers, the old man had said.

Stark's phone rang. It was Sarah. He didn't answer. Couldn't. Not here. Not now. Yet he knew that Sarah called only when she felt she absolutely must speak to him and when a text would not convey what she needed to address.

The telephone rang.

King eyed him.

Stark excused himself and took the call over at the edge of the hallway.

"Hey," he said, "what is it?"

"Your father," she said, her voice sharp, winded.

Stark's blood went cold. He had not yet told Sarah about his father waiting for him across the street from their house, fresh out of prison after twenty years. He hadn't wanted to alarm her or give her anything more to be concerned about. She had enough to deal with after Q's attack. She did know that his father was out, released on parole, and that he had left a message on their home phone for Stark. She had even spoken to him when she answered the phone. Had he called her cell, found her number somehow? Or had he already done something to get himself arrested and she'd seen it in the news before Stark could? "What about him?" Stark said.

"He was here," Sarah said.

"At the cabin?" Stark said.

"Outside. Talking to Francis."

"When? Is he there now?" Stark's heart thrummed fast, made his chest buzz with anxiety.

"No. Not now."

"Outside where?" Stark said.

"Francis was feeding the horses grass at the rail fence. He came back in and mentioned a man had been out there with him."

"You are sure it wasn't just someone who works with the horses?"

Stark wondered how his father could even know where Sarah and Francis were, unless he had followed them there. Stalked them.

And if so, what did he want? Why was he doing it?

It was a risk for his father to come onto the property. It was a private estate. It didn't have a gate or any sort of security guard at the entrance, but it was still private and most of the vehicles had to be known by the workers, trainers, and the like.

"Did you see him?"

"No."

She wouldn't recognize his father anyway. She'd never seen a photo of him. Stark didn't have any. You didn't keep photos of the man who killed your mother.

"How do you know it was him?" Stark said.

"He said he was family. Who else is family?"

"Let me speak to Francis."

"You don't believe me?"

"Of *course* I believe you," Stark said.

King looked at him, then looked away.

"He's in the shower," Sarah said. "He was all muddy."

"I want to talk to him," Stark said, his voice hard.

"Then come home."

"I will as soon as I can. What else did he tell you about the man?"

"It was your father."

"Did he say if the man told him who he was? Or give a name, even if it was a false one?"

"He didn't give a name."

"Did you ask what he looked like?"

"He said he looked like an old man."

"Did he say if he was bald?"

"He said he had a hat on."

It was interesting this man wore a ball cap. If it was his father, he might have done it to cover up his baldness.

"Did the man say anything at all to him that Francis remembered?"

"He said the horses were nice. And the cabin. Asked if he liked staying here, asked Francis his name. But Francis didn't give it. Just as we taught him."

"Good," Stark said.

"It was your father. I know it. He said Francis looked just like his own son."

Stark didn't like it. Any of it. Who was this man? Could it be his father?

"What else?"

"That's not enough for you? Get home and ask Francis yourself. When will you be here?"

"As soon as possible. But I can't get there right now."

"Why was your father even here? What does he want?"

"We don't even know it was him."

"It was. I know it. What am I supposed to do if he shows up again?"

"I'll call Jerome and have him get someone on the stable's staff to keep an eye out." Stark didn't tell her that he knew the model of the car his father was driving and could have Jerome's employee look for it on the premises and on CCTV.

Stark didn't even know if the man was his father. But he wanted to be home. Needed to be home.

King was looking at him. Now he could not tell Sarah that his father had shown up across the street from the house, saying similar things, making veiled threats. Said that the apple didn't fall far from the tree. Said he'd do anything for Stark. It was too late to tell her now—it would just terrify her even more.

"Wherever you are, drop it and come home."

"I can't."

"Where are you?"

"A crime scene."

He couldn't tell her Franklin was dead. It would alarm her. He saw now just how suspicious Franklin's death was. If he said out loud to Sarah that Franklin was dead, her immediate reaction would be to think he'd been murdered, and she would be right.

"I'll call Jerome at the house now and see if he has someone from his staff who can keep an eye on you."

———

Stark knelt beside Franklin's body. He didn't touch him. Didn't want to. There was no point. The body was stiff and cold, the eyes clouded by death. Stark wondered about Franklin's sudden retirement. He had believed that it was because Franklin wanted to duck responsibility for making Stark invent a John Doe as the perpetrator of Q's—the Tableau Killer's—crimes. The plan had been, once Q was turned over, for Franklin to publicly announce that the Tableau Killer had been killed during the attempted capture, and the corpse of a John Doe would re-place him. The grieving survivors of the victims would get some sense of closure, and the terrorized public would have peace of mind knowing that the Tableau Killer was not still out there.

But perhaps there was more to it than this. Perhaps Franklin got forced out of the FBI—a retirement he couldn't refuse.

Or he left for another reason not yet clear: fear.

But fear of whom? Of what?

"Why am I here?" Stark said. "Why was I called into this?"

"Until we can say definitely that this was an accidental death, we can't rule out anything," Hansen said.

Stark knew this, and he knew why he was here. He hadn't even realized he'd spoken aloud. He'd meant, *What happened to you to bring me here, to bring you here, to this point?*

"Do you think this has to do with the case you were working on under him?" the ME said. "The Tableau Killer?"

Hansen didn't know that the case had been about to be closed and that Q, the perp, had been caught and sent back to the program by Stark, under pressure from Franklin, instead of following expected protocol that would have seen Q booked and held in FBI custody. Breaking protocol wasn't just unorthodox. It was, in Stark's twenty years in the Bureau, unprecedented. If the public found out that the Tableau Killer had come from a covert government entity that spent millions in public funds to research something as controversial as remote viewing, the story would be met with public furor and consume the headlines for months. There would be congressional investigations, and the outrage machine would go into overdrive. The FBI would be grilled about how this government employee had gone rogue without their knowledge. It would be seen as a massive boondoggle, and neither Stark's nor Franklin's career would survive the fallout.

Stark had pushed back until he realized his career and pension were under threat from Franklin. And now, only days after Stark had gone against his own personal and professional instincts and Franklin retired early to extricate himself from any entanglement, Franklin was dead.

Franklin was not a man you'd bet on dying out of the blue. He was the epitome of the careerist in his mid-fifties who rose before the sun to hit his Peloton for an hour of rigorous cardio, do a hundred push-ups and a hundred sit-ups, drink his protein-and-veggie smoothie, and seize the day.

That didn't mean he couldn't die unexpectedly. Stark's close friend had died in his sleep at fifty-two years old. His wife had said he woke in the night to let the cat in and returned to bed mumbling to her about the damn cat. He had kissed her cheek and rolled over on his side, his back to her. When she awoke in the morning, she knew instantly: He was dead. She just knew. An aneurism.

He too had been fit, though perhaps not as athletic as Franklin. He enjoyed the couple of beers on the weekend, or wine or a cocktail socially. But compared to the general populace, he was in great shape. He exercised in some manner every day, whether with an easy forty-minute jog, a bike ride, a hike in the Blue Ridge Mountains, or even a brisk ten-thousand-step walk, and he hadn't eaten dessert since he turned forty. But there was being healthy and there was being ill, and often people could be both at once. He was healthy and fit, *except* for that tiny, nearly microscopic blood clot in his brain that neither he nor anyone else knew of until it dislodged and lodged again. Stark had suffered prostate cancer a decade ago. The diagnosis had floored him, bent his reality. He was too young to get it—forty years under the norm—and he felt fine. He was still young, and if he hadn't done a random PSA test, he would never have known he had the cancer until he felt symptoms, which by then was often too late. People asked how he found out. A blood test, he told them. Never felt a thing. He had undergone surgery—a total prostatectomy. Wore a catheter for a week, wore diapers for months, and was impotent for two years. But never, except for physical recovery from the surgery itself, had he ever once felt sick.

He didn't like to think about it. That something could grow silently, malignantly, inside you—that your own body could turn on itself and kill you.

Death did not care if you were a newborn or ninety-five years old; celebrating on the dance floor of your own wedding reception; bending down to pick up a seashell at the beach; eating a ham sandwich on the train ride to the first day of your dream job; or minutes from the doorstep of a well-earned retirement.

It was entirely possible Franklin had died of an aneurism, a heart attack, or a stroke.

Still, Stark didn't like it. Didn't like the timing of it.

Did the program fear that Franklin's retirement was a threat to it? Did it fear that Franklin would somehow expose it, exploit it, even after he had gone to such great lengths to conceal it?

Stark caught himself. He kept thinking of the program as *it*. But it wasn't some faceless, soulless corporate entity. The program was made up of human beings. Who were the few humans who actually ran the program? That was the question that needed answering. There had to be a few at the top who oversaw it, who dictated what the program did and what it did not do. What its vison was. Its intent. Its purpose. If Stark could find out who they were, he would get at their motives— and possibly the motives of those they exploited: the remote viewers. The Six.

But how?

"You don't think he died of a heart attack or a stroke?" King said to Stark.

Stark didn't answer.

"Odd," Stark said, "that he should have an accident like this now."

"Now?" Hansen said.

"He just retired."

"I hadn't heard," she replied.

Stark stepped outside, where Garnier waited on the front steps.

"I need you in here," Stark said to him.

He led Garnier into the living room.

When Garnier saw Franklin's body, his face went still.

"If you could give us a few minutes," Stark said to Hansen.

Hansen bowed out of the room.

"I need you to try to remote-view," Stark said to Garnier.

"What happened to him?" Garnier said, his voice grave.

"We don't know. Maybe you can get something."

Garnier stepped around to the other side of the coffee table and stood at Franklin's head. He closed his eyes.

His eyelids twitched.

After some time remaining still, he went rigid and his eyes opened with a start, as if he'd been awakened by a gunshot.

Stark was sure Garnier was viewing something helpful.

Garnier rubbed the back of his neck, clawed at it as if an insect had just stung him.

A strange, strangled sound escaped his throat, and his shoulders seemed to lock up.

Stark remained quiet and still. He waited for Garnier to regroup. Garnier was breathing hard, his breaths short and sharp, his face damp with sweat.

Gradually, his breathing calmed, and he stood, still rubbing the back of his neck as if it were sore from exertion.

"Something's wrong," he said. "It feels as if I'm short-circuiting. Like those cheap Fourth of July sparklers that spit hot sparks. That's what it feels like at the base of my skull, inside the back of my head. My brain. It's sizzling and there's a stiff wire skewering me, hot enough to cauterize."

Garnier closed his eyes and breathed. He opened his eyes with a long exhalation.

"Did you view anything?" Stark said.

"Nothing that makes sense."

"What did you see?"

"Gibberish. Nonsense," Garnier said.

"Describe it to me. Maybe there's something there."

"There isn't."

"I'll decide if there is or isn't."

But Stark knew that it wasn't up to him. Whatever Garnier viewed, Stark couldn't force him to say what it was. Garnier had the advantage.

Stark had to trust that what Garnier told him was accurate, that what he'd viewed was nonsensical and of no help to the case. He could not afford to make a mistake.

Stark's phone rang.

It was Director Valken. Valken had never called him directly. Never had reason to.

The director spoke in a brusque tone.

"I can be at the Bureau in two hours," Stark said.

"Come to my home," Valken said.

Why would he want to meet at his house?

He gave Stark the address. "Head straight here from Franklin's place."

CHAPTER 14

The long, sweeping hills leading up to the country estate remind her of a painting in which a young woman crawls through a field, looking up at a grand old house. S doesn't think the woman would ever make it up to the house, and no one in the house seems aware of the woman in the field. No one will ever look her way, and she will die there.

A metal gate stands framed between two massive rock sentries at the end of the long gravel drive.

S stops the car and looks at the gate. Has Randolph deceived her? He never mentioned a gate and had not given her a code or key for it.

Is there no way to get beyond the gate? The driveway is so long, the house can't be seen from here. It must be just over the far hill of golden grasses.

S gets out of the car. She doesn't want to be seen. Cannot afford to be seen.

She hurries to the gate. It is unlocked.

It is heavy, and when she swings it, the momentum slams it against a massive beech tree.

She brings the car up inside the gate, quickly gets out, and swings the gate shut.

She drives up over the hill and, cresting it, sees the vast, shimmering Atlantic. Overlooking a cliff stands Randolph's home—or, likely, one of his many homes. It is not as palatial as she expected. It is old and beaten by the sea and sun, but it has an ageless grandeur that, despite its unremarkable size, gives off an air of wealth.

She parks in front and goes to the door, punches in the number and takes a breath before she tries the knob. It turns. The door is unlocked. Inside, the stone foyer is cool. The alarm on the wall is emitting a steady, tiny beep. A countdown to the true alarm going off. S punches in the number and hits Enter.

The alarm keeps beeping.

She taps in the number again, and the beeping stops. The alarm's lights go red. She doesn't know whether this is good or bad. Red as in *the place has been breached*, or red as in *the alarm has been shut off*.

She waits, her heart beating hard.

The alarm doesn't go off.

Not taking any time to look around the place, she sets off straightaway toward the living area. She finds the buffet sideboard Randolph described, the low morning sun bathing the spacious room's dark wood floors in a golden warmth.

She draws the top drawer open and locates the paper she sought, set between the pages of a Murakami novel. It is a letter of invitation to be a keynote speaker at the Institute for the Advancement of the Human Mind for one week. There is no mention of the program. The honorarium for the week is $100,000, with all expenses paid for travel, lodging, and food and drink. The letter is indeed signed by a Wallace Germaine and a Vivian Sadler.

S has never heard of either of them.

Randolph has been telling the truth. Nothing in the letterhead or the tone of the letter suggests this is anything less than an authentic and established research entity, perhaps even a nonprofit interested only in the betterment of society. Other speakers' names are also mentioned. A Dr. Friede. Dr. Phyllis. A pharma exec named Randall.

Sadler. That name does, perhaps, sound familiar. But why? Not the exact name but similar, as if she knows a name spelled with the same letters but in a different order—an anagram. She thinks about it, but no name comes.

The other name, Germaine, means nothing at all to her. It doesn't sound familiar or remind her of another name. Yet, they are on the letter of confirmation, and Randolph said these were the people he had met.

A phone rings. S jumps, startled. The ringing continues, shattering the quiet. S looks around, not knowing where the phone is located, but it is nearby. Close. The phone rings and rings. Each ring makes her shiver. Each silence between rings is a breath held in the hope the ringing will stop.

It doesn't stop.

She follows the sound and locates the phone sitting on an end table next to a sofa behind her.

The phone keeps ringing. It should have stopped by now.

It rings. And rings.

The phone is old. Ancient. A black rotary phone. It vibrates slightly each time it rings, as if frightened by its own sound.

No one in their right mind would let a phone ring when there was clearly no one there to answer it.

Unless.

Unless the person calling *knows* there is someone there to answer it. And the person calling wants to speak to them. To S.

No.

No one can know she is here.

Unless the caller is another remote viewer.

The phone rings.

It feels as if the ringing is coming from inside her head, incessant and insistent as if she suffers from some aural malady. It makes her head hurt.

The phone rings. It isn't going to stop.

It is going to keep ringing as long as she is here.

So, she needs to get what she came for, and leave.

She digs around in the drawer, looking for the photograph. She finds it at the back of the book. Going by the name tags, it is of Dr. Germaine with Dr. Sadler.

She cannot believe what she is seeing. She knows the man. She viewed him recently. The woman too.

It is not possible.

They are not doctors. She knows them as something else entirely, by altogether different names and roles.

These two individuals are part of the program.

S takes the photo and shuts the drawer.

The phone rings.

She picks it up.

"Hello," she says.

"Hello, S."

CHAPTER 15

Valken's suit was a shade of blue so dark it could be mistaken for black. His tie was metallic gold with a full Windsor knot at the throat, dimpled just so. He was tall, with only the slightest stubborn paunch that not even the most militant diet-and-exercise regimen could vanquish. His close-cropped silver hair gave him less of an air of a government official than of an aging punk rocker. Odd how the same cut with electric clippers could result in such varying impressions on different men: military, punk, neo-Nazi, or just average Joe trying to conceal his hair loss.

Stark wondered about Valken's directive to meet at his home. He had expected to arrive at a stately, old historic brick home with a circular gravel drive and a portico, like so many old houses out here at the edges of Alexandria. Well-kept gardens and manicured lawns. White fences and perhaps a horse stable. Instead, he stepped across the threshold of a mid-century modern—a single-level affair with abundant glass and blond wood trim, rectangular and angular, with a flat roof that reminded Stark of Finland and of the only famous architect he could name: Wright.

The inside of the place was open and expansive yet eminently inviting. The interior woodwork and floors too were blond and mirror smooth. It was the kind of place Stark expected to see two cats dozing in a patch of sun.

The kitchen cabinetry and the furniture kept up the minimalist Scandinavian look: glass and silver and grays and soft natural sunlight.

Stark wondered again why he and Valken were meeting here. He had never met with just Valken and had sat in on only a couple of meetings with him.

It perplexed him. And it worried him.

"Sit," Valken said, and nodded at a low streamlined couch with silver fabric. The couch sat in front of an impressive window overlooking a field.

Stark sat.

Valken sat across from him on a couch identical to the one where Stark sat.

"What do you make of Franklin?" he said.

"We won't know until the autopsy and the ME's report."

Valken crossed a leg over a knee. "What do you make of *him*?" Valken's face betrayed no emotion over Franklin's sudden passing. Stark had not expected one, necessarily. This was professional.

"I'm not sure I understand," Stark said.

"He put in for early retirement. It was quite sudden."

"I heard," Stark said.

"What do you make of that?"

"I was surprised by it, sir."

"Any idea why he might put in for retirement two years early?"

Stark wondered if Valken was testing him, if Valken knew that Franklin had coerced Stark into releasing Q back to the program. Perhaps it had even been Valken's call, and Franklin had only been passing it down to Stark. If Valken was trying to trap Stark, it was not going to work. Stark learned long ago that the bare truth was the best tactic. It wasn't a tactic at all.

"Sir, if I might," Stark said. "I believe Franklin's death. The timing of it is . . . convenient."

"Convenient for whom?" the director said, watching Stark.

"I don't know, sir."

"If you don't know who his death would be convenient for, how can you posit that it is convenient at all?"

So, this was the director's style: to push back on theories, to challenge agents to think through their theories, to see an investigation or evidence from every possible angle.

"Sir, within days after he retires unexpectedly—days after he has me turn this Q over to the program—he falls and hits his head?"

"Who's Q? What program?"

"The program, sir," Stark said, confused. "The organization that Gilles Garnier came from to assist me as a consultant in the case. Perhaps you know the program by a different name."

"Gilles Garnier?" Valken said.

The director of the FBI had better things to do than remember the name of every consultant assigned to hundreds of open investigations; in most instances, he wouldn't be involved at all. Except that Garnier had met with Valken in person and been assigned to the Tableau Killer case by Valken himself. Still, this was months ago. It was possible Valken did not recall Garnier's name.

"Garnier, sir," Stark said. "He was assigned to me on the Tableau Killer case."

"You act as if I should know this."

"He was assigned by you, sir," Stark said. "After he met with you at the outset. You signed off on him. Sent him my way."

"I don't think so," Valken said, troubled.

"Sir. My understanding is that Garnier was sent from the program to you, and then you sent him to work with me on the Tableau Killer investigation." Stark was aware he was repeating himself, but he didn't know what else to say.

"I don't know who this Q and Garnier are," Valken said. "Or anything about this program. And I'm too busy to guess. So, tell me."

"Gilles Garnier is from the program, a government entity that researches and works with . . ." About to say it aloud, he felt foolish. "Individuals who can visualize people and events from a remote location and—"

"Stop." Valken held up a palm. "Remote viewing, I have heard of. It's the stuff of CIA lore from the 1960s. LSD tests, ESP, and remote viewing. Stargazer. It's not something I would ever involve myself in or suggest being used in a case, not even in a consulting capacity. I certainly wouldn't call on an individual of this ilk to help. It's nonsense."

Stark was vexed, and more than a little disturbed. Something inexplicable and troubling was going on here.

"Perhaps it's known to Garnier as the program, but to the FBI it's known as something else," Stark said.

"Do you think, Agent Stark, that I wouldn't know about such an entity under *any* name? It was once, eons ago, called Stargazer, I believe. But do you think I'd ever entertain consultation from that realm? The very notion is absurd. Who is this Garnier, and how did you come to understand that he had met with me?"

"He helped me break the case. Apprehend the perpetrator. Q."

"When?"

"You're not aware, sir?"

"This is what I am telling you. Do you suddenly not understand plain English, Agent Stark? The question is, *why* am I *not* aware? You claim a high-profile suspect was apprehended and arrested, and it hasn't been brought to my attention, and I haven't seen it in any media?"

"He wasn't arrested, sir."

Valken stood with a single abrupt motion and moved to the window behind Stark.

Stark was unsure what to do. He couldn't see Valken behind him without craning his neck around. It was an awkward situation.

Stark stood.

Valken had his back to him, looking out the window.

"I thought you knew all about this," Stark said. He was no longer just worried or confused. He was frightened. "I was under the impression that everything had come at your direction, sir."

"'Everything,' meaning what?"

"How it was all handled."

"How all *what* was handled, Agent Stark?" Valken turned and faced him. His face was red with indignation. He was furious.

Stark had no idea how Valken didn't know about any of this. Who, if not Valken, had directed Garnier to work on the Tableau Killer case?

And now Stark had to tell him Stark had given a murderer back to a program that Valken knew nothing about until this very moment. He didn't know where it would lead, but he had to tell him. He had no choice.

"Franklin directed me to turn Q back over to the program, sir."

"Who is this Q?"

"He was in the program, with Garnier. He's the Tableau Killer and also one of six remote viewers from the program."

"Let's forget for a second this remote-viewing consultant I've never heard of. You're telling me you had a suspect for the Tableau Killer case apprehended and Franklin told you not to have him charged and booked and processed. Instead, he told you to what? Turn this subject over to this *program?*"

"He'd made an arrangement for me to do it. To drop him off and turn him over."

Stark told Valken everything: about the arrangement to use a John Doe in place of Q, and how they would put it out to the media that the Tableau Killer had been killed during his arrest, and thereby give the survivors and victims' families some relief.

Valken paced the room, shaking his head, arms folded across his chest.

He stopped pacing and pointed at Stark. "And you didn't question this arrangement?" Valken said.

"I did, sir. I resisted it and countered it for all the appropriate reasons."

"But?"

"He was my superior, sir."

"Chain of command can be broken in certain circumstances."

"I felt I was in no position to break chain of command. To question his motives."

"It's a predicament."

"Yes, sir, it was."

"Not *was*, Agent Stark. *Is*. It *is* a predicament. For me. For the Bureau. For you. You understand that. You've put a dangerous, violent offender into the custody of people, some program, whose existence I had no knowledge of five minutes ago. I will get agents on it, to gather intel. To find out if it exists and, if so, where it is located. But you claim you've been working with an individual I sent to work with you. If he's from this supposed program, have *him* tell you where it's located. Why do you say I directed him to work with you?"

"He said he'd met you. As did Franklin."

"Franklin said that this individual and I met? In person?"

"Or at least, Franklin never contradicted him. Garnier said as much in front of him."

"I'd like to know why this Garnier lied to you about meeting me. We need to know who he really is, who he really works for. Do you understand how important this is?"

"I do," Stark said, though he wasn't at all sure that he did understand just how this had happened, or how far the fallout would reach. But something was very wrong.

"You will report directly to me from here out on this case. Understood?"

It was.

"I won't go through the normal channels concerning your disregard for protocol in allowing a suspect to be released from custody. We must get this suspect back. That's the priority, getting this Q back. You need to find out from this Garnier where this so-called program is located. We will deal with him and the fallout from this as it affects your career once we see this through."

Stark had no idea where Q was or how to get him back. He didn't even know who he'd released him to, that day on the side of the road.

"The sudden death of Franklin is a priority as well," Valken said. "Something's not right here. I agree. We'll see what the autopsy reveals. But I want you to appreciate how profoundly undermining of the process of justice your breach of code was and remains. You should have recognized that Franklin's entire approach was lacking in merit and working outside the system. And that the appropriate step for you to take would have been to bring Franklin's behavior to his direct superior, who would have brought it to me. You yourself are not out of the woods. You are on notice. Everything from now on must be done to the letter. And it goes through me. The first thing we need to do is get this Q back. And you need to keep an eye on this Garnier. Whoever he really is might not be at all what you've been told. It's possible there is no *program*. It's possible he's quite dangerous. Keep him close; keep a report on him. I'll tell you when to bring him in to me. And I need a report on Q and this program and where the investigation is now."

"There are others who were at the program," Stark said. "Four others besides Garnier and Q, and at least one of them, as we understand it, is committing murders now."

"Find Q. Find them all. Goddamn it. A lot more than just your career depends on it."

CHAPTER 16

"We need to get Q back," Stark said to Garnier. "You need to tell me where the program is located."

"I don't know," Garnier said. He rubbed the back of his neck and winced. At the sink of his motel efficiency, where Stark and King met to speak with him, Garnier filled a plastic cup with water and drank from it, grimacing. He tugged the curtain on the window beside him, drawing it closed, the room becoming dimmer than it had been.

King glanced at Stark. She seemed a bit unnerved by Garnier, and Stark could not fault her. "How can you not know where you lived out your childhood and young adulthood?" she said to Garnier.

"We were never told where we were." Garnier groaned. "I need something for this blasted headache and neck pain."

"You never asked where you lived?" King dug around in her backpack and produced a bottle of ibuprofen, handed it to Garnier.

"I never thought to ask where I lived," Garnier said, and with a scowl, he washed down a half dozen of the tablets. "Why would we?"

"Well, how about curiosity, for a start?" King said. "For a sense of identity, your place in the world."

"The program *was* the world. Until we were teenagers, and they began to groom us for missions focused on the outer world—what I heard was called the Wilds—we knew nothing beyond the campus of the program." He sat on the edge of the bed and put his head between his knees and moaned.

"God, my head," Garnier said. "My neck. It feels like there's something chewing at my brain stem. Ants or spiders crawling and biting." He went rigid, his eyes wide. "Jesus."

King gave Stark a grave look. He had seen Garnier in pain before and hoped it would soon pass, as it always had. Yet now Stark wondered if Garnier's pain was real, or merely affected to deflect Stark's questions about the program's location. Who was he? Where did he come from? And why did he and Franklin, who was now dead, tell Stark that Garnier had met Valken in person?

"Give him a minute," Stark said.

Garnier rocked in place, rubbing his neck and wrapping his arms around the back of his head. After a spell, he straightened up. His face was leached of color, his body slack. He nodded for Stark to continue.

"What did it look like?" King pressed.

"We were near the mountains," Garnier said, winded. "East of what I came to believe were the Rockies. There were beautiful mountains to the west. Jagged peaks, snowcapped even in July."

"That's good; that narrows it down," King said.

"To about ten thousand square miles," Stark said.

"What do you remember of it?" King said.

"There was a helipad. Our own. Helicopters used it occasionally."

"Okay," King said, and made a note.

"The mountains were to the west," Garnier said. "We were in the foothills, in a valley, nearer the plains. There was nothing else. No other structures or buildings within sight. Only our buildings, on campus, as it was called. There was a one-lane dirt road that left the campus. Beyond the fence there was nothing man-made except the helipad."

"Fence?" King said.

"The perimeter of the entire campus was fenced. A tall wire fence with razor wire at the top."

"What did the mountains look like?" King said. "Anything in particular strike you? Stand out?"

"They were mountains. They looked the same as any other."

"They don't," King said. "The Cascades are nothing like the Tetons, which are nothing like the Appalachians. Mountain ranges and mountains are distinct. Singular."

"I suppose."

"It's not a supposition. It's fact. So, think," King said.

Stark appreciated how King pushed Garnier.

"Draw a map of the campus," Stark said. He looked around the motel room, opened a nightstand drawer, and took out a notepad and a pen. "The buildings—how they were spaced, sizes and shapes of each. As best you can."

Stark handed Garnier the pad and pen.

"Was there any structure that stood out?" King said. "Draw them."

"Are you planning on going there?" Garnier said.

"It's likely Q is there. And it's at the root of all this," Stark said. A vehicle pulled up out in front of the room, tires crunching on gravel. A door closed. The shades were drawn so there was no way to see who it was. Stark waited. He heard a child shout and continued.

"It's where all this began. An entity that had you and the others essentially under their control your entire childhoods. The program had every reason to believe Q was the Tableau Killer, that he was the one murdering families, and they did nothing to notify the authorities directly but instead sent you covertly, all the while keeping you in the dark. They tried to cover their tracks that it was one of their own doing this. Remove themselves from the equation and avoid accountability."

"Except it's not an entity," King said. "Or rather, it is, and it isn't."

"How do you mean?" Stark said.

"It's an entity, but it's made up of human beings who made choices, who *chose* to do what they did. What they continue to do. It's made up of individuals, and these individuals need to be held to account."

She was preaching to the choir, Stark thought. And she was dead right.

She said to Garnier, "Think. Close your eyes. And relax and think." The tone and volume of her voice reminded Stark of a hypnotist. "Think. Remember . . . Or remote-view it, if that helps."

Her voice was calm and steady and smooth, a deep, slow river. Her voice put Stark in a state of reflection. His mind drifted to memories of his father waiting for him outside his house just a few days ago. The old man had just been released from prison after doing twenty years for murdering Stark's mother. He stood next to his car, his big arms folded across his chest with an air of a challenge.

Stark hadn't laid eyes on him in twenty years, since the one time he visited him in prison. He wanted nothing to do with the man or with what he had done, both to Stark's mother and to Stark himself. It was unforgivable. As a boy, Stark had tried for a spell to forgive, felt somehow obligated to forgive his father. He had spent much of his late teenage years searching deep inside himself for a grain of empathy. He found none. To find empathy, one had to put oneself in the other person's position, know that position, and Stark could not. If he had been able to do such a thing, it would have meant he had the same darkness in him that his father had. He had no such darkness in him. There was not the tiniest sliver of him that could relate. And he was glad for that.

He could not forgive, but he had tried to forget and had managed to do so quite well: forget it all. Forget the days leading up to her disappearance, then the discovery of her body, then the police knocking at the door and taking his father away. He'd buried it. Submerged it all as his father had made him submerge his mother in Jewel Lake. He'd forgotten it all until his father's recent parole made it rise again to the surface.

"Careful," the old man had said just a few days ago across the street from Stark's home. "The apple doesn't fall far from the tree. I tell you this to try to protect you, as I always did."

His arrogance and utter detachment from reality were galling. As if the old man were trying to warn Stark, give him sage advice, intimating Stark possessed the same darkness to commit such a crime.

"Can you think of anything?" King said, breaking Stark free from his reverie.

Garnier had his eyes closed and was grinding his teeth and groaning terribly. Stark didn't know if he was trying to remote-view, or if he was simply in pain. Or neither. There was no way to know.

"A fire tower," Garnier said. His eyes remained closed, and he dropped his head between his knees again, as if he were trying to keep himself from becoming seasick.

He held one hand limply up, in a gesture asking for a moment to try to collect himself.

When he spoke again, his voice was weak and slow. "In the distance, atop a peak. I never paid attention to it. It always registered as a tree that had grown taller than those around it. Until I saw a glint, like sunlight reflected by a mirror, coming from it. And my eyes, my brain, finally registered what it was. Strange. Once I saw it for what it was, I wondered how I could ever have thought it was a tree in the first place. It was quite clearly a fire tower."

"You saw what you expected to see," King said. "Your brain expected trees, so until you were made to focus on it, you never truly saw it. That's why eyewitnesses are unreliable."

"A fire tower in the foothills," Stark said. "What else?"

Garnier held his hand up again.

In a moment, he spoke. "The higher peaks, the rugged ones, were above tree line, clearly. Newer mountains, jagged rock."

"How many peaks?" King said.

"Five? Six? I don't know." Garnier paused, head down.

"What did they look like? Were the peaks close together?" King said.

"Close together. One had sort of a double peak. That's why I said five at first. It was the same mountain but with two summits. Like it had once been one huge peak but cracked in half."

"Good," King said. "How far were they from this campus?"

"I have no idea."

"Guess," Stark said.

"Ten miles?"

"So probably thirty," Stark said. "To most people who've never bothered to calculate a distance from mountains, it's common to vastly underestimate the distance."

"So. A fire tower," King said. "Six peaks but five mountains. Twenty to thirty miles west of you. Snowcapped even in summer. We're getting somewhere."

Garnier collapsed to the floor.

———

"I don't like how that sounds," Garnier said.

He had woken in the emergency room, taken to the hospital by ambulance after he passed out and Stark called 911.

Now he sat in a doctor's office after undergoing X-rays and other imaging tests in a dreamlike fog, dissociated from it all. He had vomited twice in a little blue bag.

A doctor about Garnier's age adjusted his white coat as he sat on a stool beside the table where Garnier lay.

The doctor looked at the images in his hand, then at Garnier. "I don't know how else to say this," he said. "The X-rays we took of your neck looked at first like some sort of filaments or fine wires, or implants of some sort that had been placed inside you. But on closer examination, they're none of these. That is, you haven't ever had any sort of implant inserted in you, have you?"

"Not that I'm aware of." Garnier offered a pale smile. He looked at the fake skeleton hanging from a rod in a corner of the room. This was inside everyone, holding them up—the scaffolding of the body.

"You'd be aware, I'm sure," the doc said. "I noted the scar at the back of your neck. How did you get that?"

"I don't know," Garnier said.

The doctor appeared puzzled. "It's not an insignificant scar," he said. "You must know how you came by it."

"I was told it was from an injury when I was a toddler, perhaps eighteen months."

"What kind of injury?"

"I fell and struck myself, I think they said."

"Your parents told you this?"

"I . . ." Garnier paused. "A doctor told me. My parents—I didn't know them."

The doctor cleared his throat, shifted on the stool, a square window behind him. The window was bright with sunlight that hurt Garnier's eyes. "Okay. Well, it must have been quite a serious fall. If that's what happened. It appears to me to be a scar from a deliberate slice. I can't help but determine, after looking at all the imaging and having several colleagues—specialists—look at them as well, that the scar and the images we see of these . . . what look like tendrils, are related. Except . . ."

"What?" Garnier said.

"The filaments or tendrils appear to be organic."

"I don't understand," Garnier said.

"They seem to be a part of you. Growing from you, grown *by* you, by your own body."

Garnier rubbed the back of his neck.

"I believe the scar isn't the result of any injury," the doctor said. "Actually, my colleagues and I can categorically state that it is not. It is an incision. Made not with the intention of implanting wires or filaments in you, but of cutting into you to try to extract, to cut out, excise, whatever is growing in you."

"Cancer," Garnier said.

"No. Whatever we are to label them, they are benign, harmless. And while they are a part of your body, grown by your body, they are not—how do I put this? They are not necessarily *of* your body."

"You've lost me," Garnier said, fear rising in him. Fear and . . . anger. His entire life, he'd been lied to—one long betrayal.

"It's not clear if these tendrils are a part of you, or an organism foreign to your body that is using your body as its host. It's unclear."

"A parasite?" Garnier said, and touched his neck with his fingertips.

"If you like, but my colleague believes it was always there, inside you."

"I was born with a parasite in me?"

Garnier stopped. "Could you . . . could you pull the blind on that window," he said, shielding his eyes. "The sunlight—it's really bright."

The doctor appeared confused, but he stood and lowered the blind, then sat back down.

"We're not certain what they are," he said. "We've never seen or read anything like this. Whatever they are—however they got there and however long ago—they are not man-made."

"Someone tried to cut them from me. You think this is why I have the scar?"

"Tried and failed, at least in part. If you look closely, you'll see those tiny white specks."

The doctor showed Garnier the image, pointed to the white spots. Garnier nodded.

"More imaging needs to be done," the doctor said. "I'd like to have you admitted to the hospital, to be seen by specialists and undergo extensive—"

"I don't need to be admitted."

"Mr. Garnier, I've never seen anything like this. Not in any book or case study, or . . . These you see here, these white specks, are the remnants of microscopic stumps of those stalks or tendrils or whatever they are."

The doctor rose and put the image up on the light board and blew up the image, zoomed in.

There were dozens of them.

"We think the scar is so pronounced because many incisions were made over time, the tendrils cut back many times, as if they were weeds."

Garnier felt faint. "That's not possible. I'd know if someone operated on me like that repeatedly, sliced me open at the neck and tried to cut things out of me."

But even as he said it, he knew it wasn't true. It was possible someone had done it to him, and he knew when.

"You have no recollection?" the doc said.

"None."

"Who is your primary care?"

"Primary care?"

"Your physician, your doctor?"

"It doesn't matter."

"It's important we speak to someone who has seen you before, cared for you before—someone who knows your history. The tendrils are small but not delicate. It appears that each time they grow back, they come back thicker and stronger and more resilient, and it also appears that they grow from the spinal column up to the base of your skull, the brain. They have taken deep root. We'd like to communicate with your primary care to see what they have on your background, and then have you admitted to conduct more imaging and study."

"No." Garnier rose from the table. "Just cut them out. Cut them out for good. Now. Right here. Now."

"I'm not equipped to do that," the doctor said, seemingly alarmed.

"Slice me open and cut out the roots!" Garnier said.

"Please, calm down, Mr. Garnier. You need to take it easy."

"No more studies," Garnier shouted, and stood up. "No more lab rat. No more submission. Cut them out."

"I can't do that. Certainly not here. I don't know if anyone can, not without risk of severe damage to—"

Garnier stripped off the johnny and put on his shirt. He rubbed his neck. It was more painful than ever.

"Mr. Garnier, please. I'd like to pursue this and help you. There is something not right with—"

Garnier shoved past the doctor. "No more."

He hurried down the narrow hospital corridor, his shoes squeaking on the gleaming floors as the doctor behind him shouted, "Mr. Garnier! Mr. Garnier, please, you are in no condition—"

The doctor's voice cut off abruptly as the elevator doors closed behind Garnier.

CHAPTER 17

Garnier couldn't sleep. The base of his skull felt as if it were being pried open along its seams. The pain was acute and bewildering, but it was not the sole reason he remained awake.

This case—all he had seen and learned and endured since he was brought on—had led him here, to this profound confusion about who and what he was and about his ability to remote-view.

He walked in circles in the darkness of the motel room—five steps from the nightstand to the far wall, five steps back. He needed darkness. Light only sharpened the pain in his head and hurt his eyes. And he didn't want to see himself in the motel mirror either. He felt ancient, as if he had aged in a way that accounted for more than just years, more than merely time in this body.

Garnier.

X.

Gilles.

His names were given him by others, just as any human being was given a name that they had no power to accept or decline. They had no agency regarding the word that would define them.

X.

Gilles.

Garnier.

When Q had mocked Gilles's name that night in Stark's home, Gilles had not known what he was talking about. He hadn't known that he had been named after Gilles Garnier, a French serial killer from the 1500s who believed he was a werewolf. He was *known* as the Werewolf of Dole, a man who killed and cannibalized several children, eating their thighs and stomachs and bringing their legs home to his wife. A man who claimed he was confronted by an entity one night while he hunted food for his wife and himself, who were hungry. The entity gave the namesake Garnier an elixir that would change him into a wolf, enabling to hunt more easily. He went on to hunt and kill the children, some of whose bodies he tore apart with his teeth and hands.

Whoever in the program had given Garnier his name had to know of the original Gilles Garnier. It was no coincidence. They had thought so little of Garnier as a child and had such callous disregard for those children who were murdered five centuries ago that the name was a joke to them. What was behind their giving him this horrendous name? He wasn't violent. He wasn't like Q or S. He was angry and distraught. The more he thought about what had been done to him—his entire young life manipulated in the name of servitude to the program, being told it was for the good while being denied a real childhood with a real family—the angrier he became. He had been created for a purpose, experimented on. He was property.

So why had they given him the name X when he was young? What kind of name was X? Or Q, or S, or the other three?

To their ears, the letters *sounded* like names, just as many words sounded like letters and letters sounded like words or names. *B, D, J,* and *K* could be heard as *Bea, Dee, Jay,* or *Kay. C* as *sea. G* as *gee. I* as *eye. O* as *oh, P* as *pea, Q* as *cue, R* as *are, T* as *tea, U* as *you.* So, to Garnier and the others, living with the only names they had ever known was nothing unusual. Now, though, he saw the names for what they were: not names at all but markers assigned to them. They might as well have been given serial numbers, like prisoners. He could as easily be #1287234789 or #309483.

That was what he had been: an unwitting prisoner.

So why let him go into the world?

No one knew he existed. He would never have been missed or looked for if they'd kept him on campus. He would never have known that the world outside existed. They didn't have to see that he was educated by MIT, didn't have to enlist him to work with the FBI.

They were using him. They had been using him all along, and he had thought he knew why: to find the rogue remote viewer, Q. But that was clearly not the only reason. S was out there too. And perhaps V as well.

Garnier had dismissed Q's words as those of a manipulative lunatic who wanted Garnier to side with him, wanted to convince Garnier that Q's motives had some bearing in reality.

Q had told Garnier that the time would come when Garnier could no longer bear the pain in his head, as Q hadn't been able to bear his either—a time when Garnier would do anything to stop the pain and be able to remote-view again. Garnier had thought Q mad. But those few weeks ago, Garnier had only begun to know the pain. With each blink and breath now, as he sat in the dark, the pain intensified in exponential magnitude, with an unbearable pressure building and the sensation that the stem of his brain was being gnawed by scores of tiny, needle-sharp teeth.

He needed to get rid of the pain.

He needed to be able to remote-view again.

He was, he believed, in withdrawal. Q had been right. The surge of endorphins and adrenaline that overcame him, the release of dopamine in his brain when he remote-viewed, was unparalleled by any other experience in his life. He craved the intoxication of it, the power of it, craved being able to see with his mind what others could not.

He wanted it to never end. It was his identity, his life and purpose. He could give up the program, but not remote viewing.

He didn't belong anywhere. He had no parents. No siblings. No friends. He was not a part of this world. He had only overseers, enablers, handlers, and exploiters, all to fulfill part of the program's endgame. But what *was* their endgame?

Q knew. Q had told Garnier the truth.

Garnier felt whatever was inside him pricking at the base of his skull.

He scratched at it, picked and clawed at it. The more he scratched, the more it itched and aggravated him, like a nasty bugbite.

The ER doc had refused to cut into him and determine what it was, excise it from him then and there, and he had no one else to turn to. Except himself.

If the pain didn't abate soon, he would have to slice into his own flesh and somehow cut out whatever was inside him. In the meantime, he needed to dull the pain as best as he could with the prescription given him and hide from Stark just how excruciating it was.

He could feel it at the base of his neck. It felt like a seethe of microscopic ants crawling on the surface of his brain stem, biting it with their pointy little mandibles, creating sharp, bright sparks of pain. His brain itched, and he had no way to scratch it.

It had something to do with the scar. It had to. And he knew that the scar was not natural. And it was driving him mad.

For the longest time, in his youth, he had never even known he had a scar. The only way for him to know about it would be to contort himself with two mirrors and see the back of his neck, or for someone else to see it. And he and the other five had no opportunity to see each other's scars. The scars were located low enough on the neck that a shirt covered them. Each of the six had their own bathroom, so they never changed in front of each other. In the summer, there was no place, or time in the schedule, to swim or sunbathe. Garnier hadn't discovered the scar until he was seventeen.

He'd gone to see the assigned physician for his yearly exam and had been wearing a johnny. There were two mirrors, on opposing walls, and he chanced to catch a glimpse of the scar in a reflection of a reflection. The angle had been just right so that he could see the back of his neck clearly for an instant. In seventeen years, he had never noticed the scar. He stood closer to the mirror to get a good look. It was tricky to get a full view, but there was no mistaking it. It was a scar in the shape of a star, as if he'd been branded with the tip of a large heated Phillips screwdriver.

When his physician returned to the room, Garnier had asked, "What's this on my neck?"

The doc barely shrugged. "A little scar of some sort."

"Can you take a closer look?" he had asked.

The physician looked at it for a second. "It's a scar."

"How can I have a scar and not know about it?" Garnier asked.

"You probably injured yourself when you were a toddler or a baby. Too young to remember the incident. Don't let it worry you. It looks benign."

But he had let it worry him. He'd kept a close eye on the scar, looking at it using two mirrors, each morning and evening.

One day, not long after, he fell sick and was laid low with a fever and achiness, headache, and exhaustion. He found himself bedridden for days, drifting in and out of deep, hallucinatory sleep. In the course of his illness, he abandoned monitoring the scar.

When he came out of his fugue, slowly awakening from days of intermittent sleep, he was slow to return to his routine. It must have been a good week before he had his legs under him again. Only then did he remember to check the scar.

It had changed. It was bigger, livid with a deep red hue.

When he touched it, it stung, and it felt damp, as if it were secreting a liquid.

He wondered if his illness had caused an old scar to open again or . . . he didn't know what exactly.

Had something been done to it? To him while he slept? While he'd been lost in his fever?

When he showed his scar to his physician again, the doc said it looked the same. "Perhaps it is a shade pinker."

It wasn't a pinker shade. It was *red*, nearly purple. It wept, and it hurt.

"It's likely a reaction to your fever," the physician said. "It might have become irritated."

"It's secreting a liquid," Garnier said.

He showed the doctor, pressed a finger to the scar.

"It's irritated because you keep scratching at it," the doc said. "Secretion is normal if you've been pestering it. You might have been doing it without even being aware during your days in bed."

"Do you think it's possible the scar is from a new incision of some sort?" Garnier said. "One made while I was out of it with my fever?"

The doc strapped a blood-pressure cuff around Garnier's arm. "I very much doubt that."

"But it is possible?"

"Anything is possible, I suppose."

"I think it's an incision," Garnier said. "Or a fresh injection."

"Perhaps you had a minor procedure done when you were a young child. I'll check in your records and let you know if I find anything."

"I'd like to check my records myself," Garnier had said.

"That's not possible. The system is only accessible to authorized medical professionals. We can't permit anyone else access. They'd have access to anyone's records, not just their own."

"What if you access the records now and just let me look at mine? You can monitor me."

"It's a bad precedent." The doc glanced at the door. "I'll check. Real quick."

With a few keystrokes on his laptop, he was into Garnier's records.

Garnier tried to steal a look, and the doc shut the laptop.

"Yes," he said. "You underwent a minor procedure as a young child. Two years old. A removal of a bone spur on a cervical vertebra."

"May I see?"

"You ought to trust your own doctor." His voice was stern, eyes cold. "I'll print it out for you for your next visit. Make a follow-up appointment on your way out."

Except that there was no follow-up. Garnier never saw that doctor again.

Garnier had shown Q the scar.

"That's not right," Q said. "Something's very wrong."

"That's what I thought," Garnier said. "It looks like—"

Q cut him off. "I have the exact same thing. Not as nasty, but it's the same thing."

He pulled down the neck of his shirt.

Sure enough, there at the back of his neck was a scar all but identical to Garnier's. Not as livid, but that seemed about the only difference.

"Mine gets itchy and raw too," Q said. "Feels like some insect with spiky legs and teeth is burrowing beneath my skin. It gets worse every couple of years, it seems."

"You never mentioned it," Garnier said.

"I thought it was just a lesion or something. Embarrassing. You didn't mention yours either."

"It's not a lesion," Garnier said. "It's a scar. My doctor said it was from something done years ago. But why is my skin still so itchy?"

Garnier wondered if the other four had the same scar and, if so, what that meant. Before he could say it, Q whispered in his ear, "I don't think we should talk about it—not here, not now. We need to be careful."

Then, in a conversational tone, Q said, "It's nothing, I'm sure. If your doctor told you it was. Nothing. And I think mine's just a bad bugbite, from a horsefly or something."

They were in the bathroom—the only place where they believed they might not be under surveillance. Even this was in doubt, but they had to risk it.

They shared a stall, and Q examined Garnier's scar closely.

"It's an incision," Q whispered. "Someone sliced you. And me."

CHAPTER 18

Q and Romeau made their way along the edge of the Forbidden Zone—a grassy area with shade trees, just beyond some low concrete structures surrounded by a chain-link fence. In his thirty years, Q had never set foot beyond the gate and into the Forbidden Zone. He believed now that they were going to, but they didn't. They kept the same pace until they were beyond the restricted area. They came to another fence with another gate. Romeau put his eyes to a lens, and the gate lock clicked open.

They entered the yard with its brick walkways, and Romeau shut the gate behind them. Q followed him down a concrete path that led them to several low, flat industrial buildings.

"Which one is the lab?" Q said.

Romeau nodded at the nearest building.

They entered a long, narrow corridor with tall ceilings. The lighting was bright and crisp. The corridor was silent but for the low hum that seemed to emanate from inside Q's skull.

They walked the corridor, passing several metal doors on either side, each painted a different vibrant color. Orange, red, purple, green, white, and black. The doors were windowless.

"Here," Romeau said, putting his palm flat against a black ID screen on a door that was painted bright yellow. The door clicked and opened.

The room was vast. It was bright and cool and spare. Q's skin prickled and tightened. The walls were white and bare and seemed to glow or to be made of some substance that was not entirely solid, like a bright bank of white fog that he could put his hand through. The walls of the room were crowded with white cabinets and counters. In the center of the room stood a massive island made of what looked like stainless steel, polished to a mirror finish so that it reflected the room around it. The effect made Q feel nauseated.

The counters were crowded with centrifuges and microscopes, laptops with enormous monitors, and a scattering of petri dishes, pipettes, beakers, and test tubes. A stainless-steel refrigerator the size of an SUV stood against the far wall, and several minifridges sat on counters or were nested among the cupboards.

A small woman, elfin with her heart-shaped face, pixie haircut, and, yes, slightly pointy ears, sat on a stool at the stainless-steel island. She was peering into a microscope, working its dial. She didn't look up when the door clicked shut behind Q and Romeau.

With her eyes still pressed to the microscope, she reached for a pipette in a stand. Her gaze shifted to a large monitor where a magnified image of a petri dish showed what looked like spermatozoa squiggling in some sort of liquid. With the pipette, she sucked up a single sperm cell. She put the pipette tip into a dish with another fluid and then inserted the spermatozoon into what looked like a white blob. Q guessed it was an egg.

With this task complete, the elfin woman said, still not having looked up from the monitor, "You can't be in here. Please exit now, both o' ya."

"I need you to do something," Romeau said.

The woman manipulated what looked like a video-game joystick and watched the monitor.

"Go through proper channels," she replied. "Fill out the necessary forms. Don't just come in here and ask me casually, as if you wanted a lift to the store. And whoever that is with you *definitely* can't be in here. Go."

"I'm here because of him."

The woman sighed and looked up. Her eyes were small. Q had expected big, wide eyes to go with the rest of the elf look. Those small, round eyes threw her whole face out of whack.

"Explain," she said.

Romeau crossed the lab to her, his loafers squeaking on the tile floor. He placed the briefcase cooler on the island.

"It needs to be tested," he said.

He opened the briefcase and showed her the vial of fluid.

"Whose is this?" she said. "His?"

"You don't need to know. You need to do a genomic sequencing test on the sample and tell me if you see anything unusual."

The woman clicked her tongue. "No," she said.

"Do it," Romeau said.

The woman flinched. "There's a lot here," she said. "It's not going to be done in a minute."

"We've got time," Q said.

"Do you have two months?"

"No. Sooner. Much sooner."

"The soonest is five days. That's if I didn't have other priorities."

"You don't have other priorities," Q said. "Not now."

"Who are you?" she said. "Who is he?"

"He's from here," Romeau said. "A different part of here. One of them."

The woman narrowed her eyes, scrutinizing Q as if she might recognize him but just couldn't place where and when.

Q wondered how long this woman had worked here in this laboratory. Years? Decades? Months? He had never seen her anywhere on the main campus, and she clearly had never seen him. They were like the two sides of a coin, neither aware of the other that helped make up the whole.

"He doesn't get to make demands of me."

"But I do," Romeau said. "You've got two days."

She laughed. "All but impossible."

"Yet possible."

"I have to shear each DNA sample. Bar code. Sequence. Analyze. We've got the most advanced capabilities on earth. Even so, two days is tight."

"Two days is what you have."

CHAPTER 19

She awoke. She didn't know where she was or why she was here. It was almost entirely dark, and there was an odor, like sour milk or vomit, that turned her stomach.

She was seated in a chair, arms resting on the chair's arms. She tried to get up from the chair and couldn't.

At first she believed her arms and legs must be bound to the chair somehow, but they were not. She could not move her limbs. It was as if she were stiff with rigor mortis. She tried to look down at her arms, but she couldn't move her head. To see them, she had to glance down. She could feel her limbs, feel her entire body. Feel the chair's arms beneath her arms, its legs against her calves, her back against its back, but she could not move. She was paralyzed yet had all the feeling as if she were not. Her heart pounded in her chest, faster and faster, like a fan switched from low speed to medium to fast, until it was whirring at a violent speed with the adrenaline of fear.

When she tried to speak, her tongue felt thick and swollen and foreign, like damp cardboard.

A bright light blinked on in front of her, its glare violent. If she had been able to move, she would have turned her head away reflexively to spare her eyes. But she couldn't, so she had to endure the harsh flashes and blooms of light that came blasting through her eyelids. The light was so close, she could feel its heat on her face. It felt as if her eyelids might burn.

The light dimmed and her skin cooled. She opened her eyes.

She could just make out a shadowed figure behind the light.

She tried to speak. The words came slow and muddied.

"Who are you?" she managed.

"I can't say. Can you say who you are?" the figure behind the light said. It was the voice of a man, or at least it sounded most like a man. She couldn't be sure. She assumed it was the voice of the man who had knocked at the door, but there was no way to be certain.

She was confused. What did this person mean? "Why am I here?" she said.

"Because of your husband."

"My husband's done nothing for us to deserve this."

"It is exactly what he *hasn't* done that brings you here. He's been . . . made aware. He's been given a choice. We shall see what he chooses."

"What in God's name are you talking about?" the woman said.

"I say nothing in God's name. But he's been given a choice between the program and you, his supposed loved ones."

"What program? What are you talking about?" Who was this man? He sounded insane, speaking about some *program*. She needed to be careful not to upset him. She had no idea what he might do to her, or to her daughter and grandchildren.

"Where are my daughter and granddaughters?"

"They're on either side of you."

She had no way to know if he was telling the truth about her daughter Molly and granddaughters Olivia and Fiona being here with her. She couldn't turn to either side to confirm it. "Molly? Liv? Fiona?" she said. She got no reply. She thought she heard a soft moan over the roaring of blood in her ears.

"Say something," she said. "Anything."

"They can't," the voice from behind the light said.

She went cold with fear. "What have you done to them?"

"The same as I did to you," the voice said. "Though perhaps I gave them too much. They seem to be slower to come out of it than you were. Give them time. But believe me—they're here. Right beside you."

She looked to each side as far as she could with her head immobilized but saw only darkness.

"Place them in front of me," she said. "Drag one of their chairs with them in it in front of me so I know."

"I can't do that."

"You can. Show me. Show me."

"You just have to believe. This is about belief, about trust. You must trust me. Without trust, you die. All of you."

"You're insane," she said, and regretted it before the words died in the air.

"Aren't we all?"

She willed herself to move, concentrated all her mindfulness on even making a pinkie tremble, but nothing happened. Nothing. How could she feel her body yet not be able to move? What had he done to her, to them?

She would rather have been *tied* to the chair than paralyzed. Then, at least, she could have rocked in it, moved, tried to escape. Twisted and writhed and raged against what bound her. Fight, at least.

"Please, are you there? Molly? Girls? Are you there?" In her mind, she was struggling, fighting, whipping her body back and forth to escape an invisible straitjacket, thrashing and kicking. Yet her body remained apart from her mind.

What had he done to her? And why? *Why?*

She heard nothing from the darkness, only the tsunami of blood rushing in her head.

"Stop," the voice said. "You're embarrassing yourself. I can smell your embarrassment."

She breathed. She could smell it. Urine. She could feel it, warm on her thighs. How could she feel yet not *move?*

CHAPTER 20

Stark watched as Garnier looked across the table at him, shifting his weight on the booth's vinyl seat. He stirred his mug of tea with a soda straw but didn't drink it. He didn't look well.

"What did the ER doc say?" Stark asked.

"Migraines," Garnier said, looking down into his mug of tea.

"Did he prescribe anything for them?" Stark said.

"He gave me some pills. He doesn't know if they will help. He said migraines are mysterious. Little is known about what causes them or what can ease the pain they inflict. Each patient is different." Garnier's voice was slow and muddy.

"You sound like hell. Look it too. I thought you looked bad before, but—"

"I feel worse than I look and sound."

Stark's cell phone rang. It was King.

He answered. "Call you right back," he said, and ended the call.

"I need to ask you something," Stark said to Garnier. He leaned in, picked up an onion ring from his plate. "Your initial meeting with Director Valken, before he assigned you to team up with me." Stark dipped the onion ring in a pool of ketchup. "How did you end up meeting him?" He ate the onion ring, wiped his salty fingers on a napkin. He had taken Garnier here alone to the Iron Horse Diner to feel him out. "Someone had to have set it up for you."

"I got a summons," Garnier said. "Why do you suddenly want to know about this?"

His speech was slow, and his eyes were puffy and red.

"From whom?" Stark said, not acknowledging Garnier's question.

"I don't know. We got them, all of us six. A summons for a job or a test, and a description of what it entailed. Very formal. A letter placed in our individual mail slots in our bedroom doors." Garnier slid his mug of tea from one hand to the other on the table but didn't take a sip.

"Was it signed by anyone?"

"Summonses weren't signed. They weren't from any individual, really. They were, essentially, from the program to a remote viewer."

"You got a slip of paper slid into your mail slot and you just obeyed it?"

"You've done the same, I'm sure."

Stark reflected on this—on what he had done for Franklin in setting Q loose, what he had done throughout his career under the catchall rubric of *chain of command.*

A bell in the kitchen window rang, and someone in the back shouted, "Order up!"

"What did this summons say?" Stark said.

"To pack for an extended operation, prepare to be gone for a spell. There was a date and time to be on the helipad."

"And no one consulted you in person on this?" Stark said.

"I was given instructions that said I'd be briefed when I landed. I didn't know where I was being sent, only that my abilities were needed."

"You didn't know it was the FBI?"

"I didn't know where or who or for what. Not until I met the director. I knew nothing about who I was to help until then and knew nothing about the investigation or the Tableau Killer until then."

"And you flew in to where?"

Garnier shook two pills from a bottle and tossed them into his mouth, sipped his tea, and scowled. He placed the mug on the table and pushed it to the side.

"Why are you interrogating me?" he said.

"Answer the questions and I'll tell you more."

Garnier leaned back against the vinyl. He looked frail.

The hostess pointed a group of teenagers toward the stools at the counter. They looked disheveled and hungover, even though it was mid-morning on a Thursday.

"I was helicoptered to a small airport," Garnier said. "A private one, I gathered—and I was flown from there on a twin prop for several hours to an even smaller, definitely private airport. I was given a ride from there. A driver was waiting for me when I got off the plane. I sat in the back of the car and he gave me a file on the Tableau Killer, an encapsulation of the investigation, and a bio on you. We drove about an hour. Out to that house. He told me I was to meet the director. And the man I met when I got there, I assumed was the director. I had no reason to think otherwise."

"What was the place like?" Stark said.

The waitress came over with a coffeepot, but Stark deterred her with a slight wave.

"It was a very grand home," Garnier said. "On what seemed an estate. Finely appointed. Very posh but tasteful. Understated. Remote, out in the countryside."

This didn't sound like Valken's home that Stark had just visited.

"This was the director's home?" Stark said.

"I assumed. It was a home though."

"Who else was there?"

"Just the director and Franklin."

"Right."

"What's the problem?" Garnier said. He sipped his tea.

Stark didn't answer. "You met Valken with Franklin in your presence?"

"Franklin was there. But not in the same room."

Stark didn't know what to make of this statement. Garnier appeared to be telling the truth; he sensed no deception. Yet he knew no reason for Director Valken to lie. Stark took out his phone and searched for the director's name, found a few images of him taken from press conferences.

One of the teenage boys, in sweats and a gray hoodie, spun around too fast on his stool and knocked a saltshaker to the floor.

"Klutz!" the girl next to him said and slapped his arm.

"What do you mean, not in the same room?" Stark said.

"I met Franklin in the other room."

"So, Franklin and the director never saw each other? Explain."

Perhaps, Franklin had been played somehow. Made to believe it was Director Valken in the other room. But why? Who arranged it? It was risky. All Franklin had to do was mention Garnier to the real Valken, and the entire scheme would unravel. Whoever set it up had to know that this was unlikely. Franklin did not report directly to the Valken. And Garnier, on paper, was no more than a consultant, even though he had played an integral role on the ground.

Stark wondered if *anything* he knew about Garnier was true. That Garnier got a degree from MIT. That he was a part of special ops. That he was part of a program at all.

Now Franklin was dead, and the director had never heard of Garnier *or* the program.

"You said Valken had you prove your remote-viewing ability," Stark said. "How?"

"He had me demonstrate, which I couldn't do now if you asked me," Garnier said.

The waitress came near the booth again with the coffeepot, and this time Stark let her fill his mug and thanked her.

"And did you?" Stark said. "Demonstrate?"

"I did."

"How?"

"He had me hold a marble vase he said was connected to a special case. If I could do what I claimed, I would see a certain other object, and he knew what that object would be. He said the FBI didn't waste time with frauds."

"And?"

"I held the vase. It took almost no time to remote-view—it was so vivid. I remote-viewed a man sitting in what I assumed was a private library—all dark wood and leather club chairs and gilded lamps and soft gold lighting. He was seated in a chair, reading a book. I described him and the library. A fit man in his fifties.

"The director pointed to an ornate wooden door behind me—a gesture I interpreted as asking me to open the door. I opened the door to the very library I'd just described and seated in the club chair was the man I'd just described. Franklin. That is how I met Franklin. He stood and introduced himself. He cut an impressive figure, as you know, with his height and his hair and how fit he was, his direct eye contact, his seriousness. I'd never laid eyes on him until that moment."

"So, Franklin saw the man you thought was the director?"

"No. When I turned around, the director was gone."

"You didn't find any of this odd?"

"With *my* upbringing? I was constantly tested. Being flown to a new locale was just part of testing my remote viewing and assimilating me into working society. I didn't know exactly why I was there until Franklin told me I was, in a sense, being loaned to the FBI for an investigation. He briefed me on the investigation, its story, and you, of course—how resistant you would be to my assistance. But that was no surprise, really."

The teenager in the hoodie now had his head on the counter, resting on his folded arms, eyes closed. The counter waitress was talking to the other teens—asking about their friend, Stark supposed.

"Did the director ever come into the room and discuss the matter with you two?"

"He didn't."

"So, they never saw each other?"

"Agent Franklin and I left the house out the library door and walked a stone path through a peach orchard, back out front. Only Franklin's car remained in the drive. The car that had brought me was gone, and so was the other car that I saw when I arrived."

"What car was that?"

"I'm not good with car makes and models. It was blue, though, and had some sort of fancy-looking silver ornament on the hood. It looked new and old at the same time. Old but sleeker. I remember the hood ornament reflected the sun so brilliantly it caught my attention."

"So, Franklin never saw the director at all?"

"I assumed he had. He mentioned that's who was in the other room, and I thought until just now that Franklin must have come in the front door as I had. But of course, he could have just as easily come in by the library door. Perhaps the director had him come in the library entrance so he wouldn't leave a trace of himself in the room where I met the director."

"Or maybe he was instructed to come in that library door so he wouldn't see that the man you both thought was the director wasn't the director at all."

"What are you saying? What is this?"

"I visited with the director," Stark said. "He's never heard of you or the program, and never met you."

Garnier leaned back against the booth and crossed his arms. "I met him. I did."

"Is this the man you met?" Stark held out his phone to show Garnier images of Director Valken.

Garnier considered the image. "It looks like him."

"*Is* it him?"

"I'm not sure."

Stark brought up a few more images from varied angles.

Garnier leaned in and studied the photos. "I'm not sure it's the man I met. I'm not sure it's the director."

"It is," Stark said. "It is the director."

"The man I met looked similar, but . . . I don't know. His hair was grayer, less silver. And I think he had a mole on his cheek and was a bit slighter of build. I don't know. This man—he could be his brother, easy. But . . ."

Stark sat with the possibilities. Why would Franklin take Garnier to meet someone who wasn't the director? Or, alternatively, why would someone set Franklin up to believe that Garnier was meeting the real Director Valken?

Stark's phone rang. It was King again. He answered this time.

"Go ahead," Stark said.

"First, I've had two agents running an algorithm using the research fields that the three victims—Friede, Phyllis, and Randall—each worked in, to calculate any overlap. We found several, but one stands out in particular. It's possible but might be a stretch."

"What is it?"

"It's a complicated field. I don't really understand enough to put it out there in layperson terms, so I'm having them write up a report we can digest. I'll have it soon."

"What else?"

"Mappers and geo-trackers and satellite experts believe they've narrowed down the location of the program to three sites: one in Wyoming, one in Montana, and one in Idaho. They're poring over satellite imagery at a granular level."

"Good work."

"Lastly, we got a positive ID on the man at the bottom of the cliff," King said. "I'm texting a photo now."

"I'll show it to Garnier," Stark said. "Keep at it."

Garnier peered at the photo. "That's him," he said.

"No doubt about it," Stark said.

"No," Garnier said. "That's *him*. That's the man I saw. That's the man I was told was Valken."

Adrenaline shot through Stark. "This is the man you thought was Valken?"

"That's who he introduced himself as."

"You're certain?"

Something was at work here that Stark didn't understand—something more sinister and complicated and far-reaching than Q's being a serial killer. He put King on speakerphone.

Garnier tapped the phone screen and zoomed in on the photo. "It's him. No mistake."

"That's not Director Valken," Stark said. "Who is it?"

"Malcolm Cutter," King said. "Fifty-seven years old, married father of three. He was an actor, mostly a voice actor for audiobooks, but he did regional theater, too, in New England, in the Berkshires for the Williamstown Theater Festival, and up in Dorset, Vermont, with a group of New York City actors who have second homes up there and like to keep their chops fresh. He did some TV work in the nineties. Bit parts: Guy in Bar, Witness Number One—those types of things. A toothpaste commercial."

"He was *hired* to play the director?" Garnier said.

"You're saying it wasn't Valken who Gilles met that day?"

"Correct," Stark said.

"Then this Cutter, the actor, I doubt he knew what was going on. We're going to speak to his wife. She's been informed of his death. We'll see what she knows."

"We were set up," Stark said. "You. Me. Franklin too. The question is, why? Whoever took the risk of bringing you on to help us find Q had to know that the Tableau Killer was Q, and they needed you to locate him or help us corner him. They had to know you had the ability to do it, and your being the person closest to him helped you dial in."

"It was someone from this program you were in," King said. "It had to be."

"That's the likeliest scenario," Stark said. *And I gave Q back to them.*

"How did the man who pretended to be the director end up dead at the bottom of that cliff?" Garnier said. "And why was he at that barn just up the hill from where the victim was tortured?"

"He saw something he wasn't supposed to see," Stark said.

"That doesn't explain why he was there to start," King said.

No. It didn't. What *was* this family man, this part-time actor, doing up at that house?

"Maybe he was paid to be there too," King said.

"To what end?" Stark said.

"I have no clue," King said.

"What about your contact, the one texting you?" Stark asked Garnier.

"He's gone silent. I tried his number, and nothing. No response."

"Give me the number," Stark said.

Garnier told him the number, and he typed it into his phone.

"We'll see if we can pick up the nearest tower he pinged off. The email IP too."

"It's encrypted."

"Nothing is encrypted for the FBI."

CHAPTER 21

"Why did you give me these samples?" the elfin scientist snaps. "Is this a joke?"

"Do I look like someone who jokes?" Q says.

"What one looks like and what one is can be two very different things," she says. "All I know is, you wasted my time with all this redundancy." She looks at Romeau. "Clearly, you're working on something at the very vanguard of what is humanly possible and beyond what I imagined, and for that I am grateful to participate. But to have me do the same test over and over, to 'compare' the samples—I don't understand why you would tie up my time and resources like this."

"I'm not following you," Dr. Romeau says.

"So, it's true," Q says. "My suspicions all this time—they weren't baseless."

"What suspicions?" Dr. Romeau says.

"I'll keep that to myself," Q says.

"What did you find?" Dr. Romeau says to the scientist.

"Ask *him*," she says, jabbing a finger at Q.

"She determined that all the samples are the same," Q says.

Dr. Romeau leans back and looks at him. "Why give her samples of the same cells?"

"It's not the same cells," Q says.

"It is," she says. "Unequivocally. It is the same."

What Q does *not* say is that while each sample is identical, each sample is from a *different* individual. He took each sample himself from each of his victims. Girls. Boys. Adults. Siblings and children and parents. Not just from one family, but from all of them. Entirely different "families." Different individuals. Yet they each had the same cells. Not clones. This is not about that. No. Because his own sample is in with the others too. His cells are the same as theirs.

Does this woman not know the history of her own field?

Does she work in such a hermetic silo? Do they all work in such a detached state that they cannot see the whole of what has been created and what is possible?

Perhaps she has been used, just as Q and the other five have been used.

"The sample," Q says. "It has been genetically edited. Correct?"

"Not just one gene—many genes. So many," she says with a note of dismay and awe.

Dr. Romeau looks stunned.

"What stands out most?" Q says. "What is the most significant edit?"

"The genes of the neocortex and thalamus," the scientist says.

"Which means?" Q says.

"These genes, in theory, regulate the imagination. Creativity. Some say dreams. Memory."

"And those genes have been edited to shut those aspects down?" Q says.

"No, no, no. Just the *opposite*. They've been edited to kick the door wide open, to remove all control. To open the imagination and creativity from a trickle to a fire hose."

"And what about the memory part?"

"Long-term memory would be curtailed significantly, perhaps to no more than six months in the past."

"How could anyone live like that?"

"Because the individual doesn't know any better," the scientist says. "It's not so drastic, really. Do you recall what you were doing six months ago today? Never mind eighteen months or two years. Other than the vaguest, most general memories, if we try to recall them, we tend to recall only the most pointed and profound of our highs and lows."

Q ponders this. It is true. He cannot recall much.

"We forget most everything. We don't have the memory to recall everything, because memory is storage and we don't have enough terabytes to store it all," she says. "Not even close. We recall only what really affects us—what sticks in our brain, is implanted or branded there because of trauma or bliss. And what we remember is often not as it occurred, which is why, say, spouses will have entirely different versions of the same event—the dates different, the year, what happened, and how. The generalities are there, but the specifics are very different, and each is convinced the other remembers incorrectly, when in fact it's more likely that they both have it wrong."

"Was there anything else?" Q says.

The scientist exhales as if to steady herself. "It's not cerebrospinal fluid," she says.

Dr. Romeau begins to speak, but the scientist cuts him off.

"It is CSF, and it isn't CSF. As I said, many of the genes have been edited, but there is something else too. Something wrong. Or, rather, unnatural."

"In what way?" Q says.

"It's not human fluid. Or rather, the best way to say it is that this 'fluid' could not possibly have come from a human. It must have come from a lab. We can't possibly edit that many genes in a living human being. It's not technologically possible. And even if it is, it's illegal and immoral."

It is worse than Q suspected.

"It came from humans," Q says. "It came from several different families. Kids and adults. One sample came from me."

"That simply and plainly cannot be," the scientist says. "The genes would have to have been edited generations ago and passed on, using germ-line hereditary editing of the ancestral embryos."

"I'm telling you the truth," Q insists. "Draw some from me right now and see for yourself. The other samples all came from different individuals. Kids and adults alike."

"Get him out of here," she says. "He's mad. I don't know what he's playing at, but—"

"What *I'm* playing at?" Q says. "Take my blood. Take it now! Take some DNA! Test my cells. Draw it and test it yourself. Right now! Right now! Put it under your damn microscope. It won't take long for you to see for yourself. And tell me, what kind of place is this? Who am I really? We each work in our own little silos, none of us knowing what the others are up to, the right hand not knowing what the left hand does, not knowing that a left hand even *exists*, only there isn't just a right and a left hand. We're an octopus. A millipede. So many arms and legs and hands, none of us even knowing the others exist until we cross paths. What are your skills used for? You edit genes. Do you even know? Are you allowed to leave here? Have you been here your whole life, like me, trained to do your one thing, honing your ability for the greater cause?"

She gapes at Q in horror.

"Did you ever think, stop to wonder, why am I here?" Q says. "Why, when the day is done, I have never gone to a home beyond those gates, to a family, a wife and kids? Why instead I retreat to a place that is little more than a closet? Why all of us do? Why we all stay here? We are made to stay. I escaped. Others were released, but they had their brains screwed up from the start. No long-term memory anymore, so no one to blame, no past to look back at and say, 'It started with them'; it started in that place, the program—because they don't remember the program and never will. Those families. That is why they wouldn't do what I asked of them in their homes. They had no idea they could do it, no idea who they really were."

"I want him out of here. *Now.*"

Q spins as Romeau moves toward him.

Q snatches a syringe from his coat pocket and holds its needle tip to Romeau's throat.

Romeau pleads, "You can trust me. You know me."

"I don't know you."

"I can tell you things and show you things. I've been used and manipulated as much as you have—more so! You have no idea."

"I have enough of an idea," Q says.

He sinks the needle deep.

As Romeau sinks to the floor, Q turns his attention to the scientist.

CHAPTER 22

The morgue was cool as always, to keep the corpse as stable as possible. It was a clammy coolness, the kind that always made Stark think of damp cave walls, deep in the dark earth. Even the smell of the place reminded him of caves, or perhaps it was tombs. There was the chemical scent, but it was buried beneath a mineral, earthen scent—perhaps the blood, or the viscera. The stainless steel and the bright, unforgiving lights gave the entire theater a cold, clinical atmosphere. Which it was. This was a place of surgical precision, of bodily sciences.

The ME, Brianna Caston, rolled the corpse out from its refrigerated cubicle. There was no way to ID the man by his face, whose fractures and torn flesh and bloat and discoloration rendered it barely recognizable as human. Stark had great admiration for the agents who could pull together a 3-D interpretation of a likeness, even with the aid of an AI program.

"I'd never know it was him," Garnier said.

"Not even his wife would. He was arrested years ago, in his early twenties. Something minor and stupid—illegal trespass at a railroad yard. But it meant we had his prints."

Garnier touched the body's shoulder with a fingertip.

"Don't do that," the ME said.

"Do we know if the fall was accidental?" Stark said. "Or was he pushed, or maybe died before the fall?"

"His toxicology was clean, so we can rule out drugs or alcohol, whether self-induced or not. And there was no cardiac arrest or stroke to indicate he suffered a seizure or was otherwise made to stumble. The fall killed him; that is clear. He sustained massive brain and organ trauma, a broken neck, a fractured skull. These injuries were instantaneous on impact. But whether he stumbled, jumped, or was pushed is unknowable."

"That's something at least," Stark said, but it was half-hearted.

Garnier touched the body again.

"I'm going to demand you leave if you keep touching the corpse," Caston said.

Garnier pulled his finger away and closed his eyes.

Caston glared at him.

"We don't have time to explain," King said. Her phone pinged and she gestured that she'd take it outside.

"I don't even want to know," Caston said. She had seen it all in her nineteen-year tenure and likely saw Garnier's behavior as a performance. Stark couldn't fault her intolerance. But she also knew Stark and knew he wasn't one to tolerate such behavior either, not without sound reason. So, she tacitly permitted Garnier to remain when she likely would have ousted him.

Garnier's shoulders and jaw went slack. A low humming sound came from down in his throat, reminding Stark of prayerful monks. Garnier bowed his head. It was then that Stark saw it: something glistening inside Garnier's ear. Stark thought it was wax at first, but it was silvery and clear, a bead of liquid. Like a teardrop. It trembled at the edge of his ear; then its surface tension broke, and it trickled out down his neck.

If Garnier felt it, he gave no indication.

His eyes moved beneath their trembling lids, flitting back and forth as if watching a tennis match from the sideline without moving his head.

He opened his eyes and blinked. His eyes were glazed, the pupils huge and staring. "Nothing," he whispered.

Caston sighed.

"You sure?" Stark said. "Didn't look like nothing."

"It's difficult with the deceased." Garnier rubbed the back of his head, then examined his fingertips. "I don't feel well," he said. His voice sounded feeble.

"You don't look well," Caston said. "Your color is gone. It happens." She was referring to a layperson being so close to a corpse—the odors, the autopsy room itself, the whole of it.

"I need to . . ." Garnier said. "I need to rest. I need to sleep. Recharge, if I can."

"I'll drop you at the motel," Stark said. "I want you to get some shut-eye. You need it. Take a day and just sleep and get back on your feet. You're no good to anyone like this."

Stark could use the time to visit Sarah and Francis for a short spell. He wanted to see them, see his wife and son.

Outside, as Stark and Garnier made their way down the steps, Garnier using the rail, King approached Stark.

"Sir, we have a missing person of interest."

CHAPTER 23

Q stands with his bare back to the vanity and holds up a hand mirror. Even with this, it is difficult to see the back of his neck clearly. He has to crane to do it, twist himself into an odd position. He touches his fingertip to the spot. He can feel it just beneath his skin—the tiny barb, the probe, whatever the hell it is.

He raises the X-Acto knife and turns his neck. He touches the sharp tip of the blade to the spot, right at the center of his scar.

The razor's tip feels cold and hard. And sharp.

He grits his teeth and presses the very tip of the blade to his skin. Pushes.

The skin splits open with little pain.

His fingers are warm and slippery with his own blood. He feels around for the barb. It isn't there. How can that be? His fingertips probe and feel something, a tiny prick. Yes, this is it. It feels like a piece of stiff wire, yet it seems to have some sort of slick coating.

He tries to pinch it between his fingers, but the blood and the slick coating of the tendril make it difficult. He needs something besides his fingers to grasp it with. He needs a tool. He goes to a drawer and finds a small rusty pair of needle-nose pliers beneath the sink.

He takes the pliers in his trembling fingers and sits up against the wall.

With eyes closed, he takes long, slow breaths to further calm himself.

"What are you doing!" a voice says. "What on earth are you *doing*?"

It is S. She has come in from the other room, where she was with that Randolph.

"I'm cutting it out," Q says. "Whatever it is. I am cutting it out of me!"

"You can't. You can't do it that way. Put that thing down. Clean yourself up."

Q sets the X-Acto knife down.

"Good," S says. "Now, clean yourself up. And we'll see what I can do about it. If you want it out, I'll try to get it out for you. But we need to do it right. I need to put you under."

She touches the back of his neck. The jolting pain is unlike any he has ever known, and it fells him.

CHAPTER 24

"Who is he?" Stark said.

"Karl Pickering," King said as she and Stark and Garnier stopped at the bottom of the steps outside the morgue. She put on sunglasses to ward off the glare of the midday sun. The purple hue complemented the blue tint at the tips of her short dreads. "A scientist, apparently—a researcher who worked for a small yet prestigious college. He kept in the shadows, out of the media, but was highly regarded by his peers. He's no longer with the college. He got major funding and took his research into the private sector with that backing. Just himself and a few assistants."

"Who's the backer?"

"John Randolph. Überwealthy, but he comes from workaday, humble beginnings. His mother was a clerk at a local hardware store; father was a high school guidance counselor. He made his fortune back in the late-nineties wave of the internet boom. He bought a thousand dollars of shares in a young online company at seven cents a share. Amazon. Today, after the splits, he owns nearly three and a half million shares at a hundred and fifty-five dollars each.

"He got lucky, and he knew it and he never lost sight of it. He is on record as saying he'd won the lottery, had done nothing exceptional to make the money he did."

A girl on a skateboard shot down the sidewalk at the three of them, swerved between them with practiced control.

"He's been a philanthropist ever since," King continued. "Quietly donating money to causes he deems worthy. He has no board to serve him; he is obligated to no one. He doesn't serve on any boards and makes no political contributions."

The three walked to Stark's sedan and got in, Garnier in the back, King in the passenger seat.

Stark started the car and eased out into traffic.

"And he funded this Pickering. What's Pickering's research?"

"It's a rather controversial field, cutting-edge. It involves technology and chemical engineering actually borrowed from the pesticide industry."

"Pesticides?" Stark said. "Explain."

"I had the same reaction," King said. She switched her shades for reading glasses, checking her notes. She was thorough and meticulous— traits that would take her far in the Bureau. "It borrows from the field of biochemistry. What is envisioned is a synthesized molecule that at- tacks cancer cells similar to how aphids feed on unwanted invasive weeds but not the valuable crop. This molecule has a *taste* for cancer cells. It seeks and destroys them. With the cancer cells gone, the molecule dies and is absorbed. There's a synthesized molecule, ERX-4, that attacks cancer cells and leaves the healthy cells alone. It's cutting-edge. When prompted, the body, in mice and rats anyway, can create this molecule on its own to attack rogue cells and leave the healthy ones alone. The technology to create it is what Randolph was backing."

She swiped her fingers on the tablet to bring up more notes.

"According to transcripts I found online from past seminars around this field, he hopes his funding will one day help with cancers, MS, and autoimmune diseases. He was on his way to a conference in Vail, to be a guest speaker at a symposium for the Institute for the Advancement of the Human Mind and speak to donors about his research."

"He looks familiar," Garnier said, leaning over between the front seats as King held up the tablet. She enlarged the photo. Garnier studied it more closely. "I've seen him," he said.

"In person?" King said.

"He visited Stargazer."

"When?" Stark said, staggered by the revelation. "Are you sure?" He pulled the car over into a convenience store parking lot. He turned in his seat to face Garnier.

Garnier seemed to know or recognize most of the individuals involved in the case. Stark didn't like it. He didn't like that Garnier seemed central to the very case he was supposed to be helping them solve. Was Garnier aware of how he fit into all this, or was he oblivious? "Why don't you tell how you know this person too," Stark said.

"I met him years ago, but it's him," Garnier said. "He had more hair and wasn't going gray. He was heavier then. He looks trim now. But it's him. No doubt."

"Did you speak to him?" King said. Stark could tell by the interrogative tone of her voice and by the way she sat up straighter when she turned to address Garnier that she too had her radar up. She too sensed something amiss.

"We were forbidden to interact with visitors," Garnier said.

"Do you know why he was there?" Stark asked.

"No idea," Garnier said. "He would have been entirely unmemorable—just another inconsequential visitor that I registered simply as *old*. I never paid him any mind until . . ."

"Until what?" King said.

The car was warm from sitting in the sun. Stark turned on the AC. King shifted and removed her thin black leather jacket.

"I was cutting behind the lecture hall. I was late for some tests. Tardiness was not tolerated. Abidance with the regimented life was impressed on us since before we could remember. But I had woken feeling sick that day. I did my best to collect myself. Splashed cold water on my face and hurried and took a shortcut through the back of the lecture hall.

"We were supposed to stay on the stone paths. Shortcuts were cheating. I was nervous about being caught, but I figured it was better to take the risk of the shortcut and be on time—or not too late, anyway—than to be very late.

"That's when I heard someone shout. I looked to see Dr. Romeau and this Randolph in a loud but amiable exchange. Randolph was shaking his head with vehemence and pointing a finger at Romeau. I clearly heard him say, 'This will change the world. Forever, and for good!' Romeau put his arm around Randolph's shoulders as they walked away. I never saw Randolph again."

"What was his lecture about?" Stark said.

"Something to do with neurons or molecules, I'm not sure."

"You have no idea what they were talking about?" Stark said.

"None whatever," Garnier said.

"What does this have to do with us? Our case?" Stark said, impatient. Clearly, this Randolph had to have something to do with the case, since he'd been at the program; and Garnier, if he was to be believed, had seen him.

"He's been missing for thirty-six hours," King said. "He was last seen in a café in Red Canyon, Colorado. He was scheduled to speak at a conference in Vail, for the Institute for the Advancement of the Human Mind. He never showed, and his car is still in the lot across from the café, ninety miles east."

"Why did you think this Randolph's disappearance involved us?" Stark said. It was clear to him that the disappearance involved their case, but only because he'd just learned that Garnier had seen the man before, at the program.

"It seemed to me that he was perhaps connected in some way due to his background as a researcher—his type of research," King replied. "And men like him don't often just go missing."

It was good work on King's part to see a possible connection, one that was now confirmed. Stark was impressed.

"Tell me more," he said.

"A witness said she saw Randolph interact with a woman in the parking lot. He seemed to be having car trouble. The local police have impounded the car. They're scouring it and checking to see if there is indeed a mechanical problem, if it can start on its own or not, and if not, why not."

"What else did this witness say?"

"The woman was in her thirties, she guessed. Skinny to the point of anorexia. She looked 'strung out'—her words. Her face was somewhat hidden by big sunglasses and a neck scarf. There's footage of her in the café. She leaves shortly after Randolph leaves."

"Follows him?"

"It might be coincidence. A lot of people park in that lot to go to the café. The witness said it's possible the man got in a car with the woman."

"What kind of car?"

"A *car* car, meaning not an SUV or pickup. Could be a four-door or a two-door. It was white."

"Of course, the most popular color vehicle there is," Stark said. "So. She's not sure if she saw a man, with a woman she can hardly describe except that she's skinny, get into a car of the most popular color that's maybe a two-door and maybe a four-door. How can she be sure it was even Randolph?"

"He stood out. He was dressed in a peach ascot, seersucker jacket, and derby cap. He was supposed to arrive in Vail and check in at the Sonnenalp by two p.m.," King said. "He was due to speak the next day and expected at a cocktail party that evening. He never showed and he never checked in. He hasn't responded to any texts or calls, and his phone no longer pings. It's dark."

"Is he married?" Stark said. "Family? Have they heard from him?"

"A wife and a daughter, two grandkids. The thing is, sir, they seem to have disappeared too."

Shit, Stark thought. Another family. But this one was *missing*. Not tied up and slain in their home. "All of them?" he said.

"Yes, sir. The state police visited their vacation home in Maine where they were staying, to inform the wife of the abandoned car and see if she'd heard from him or knew of his whereabouts. They found no one at the house, despite there being two cars in the driveway, and a pot of sugar syrup scorched black on the stove, which was still on. A carton of ice cream melted on the island."

Stark wondered what was at work here.

"It would have to be at least two people behind the abductions," King said, "if they were abducted at all, one in Colorado and the other in Maine and happening just hours apart."

"It could be that he was abducted," Garnier said. He'd been so quiet, his voice startled Stark.

"And his family abducted for some sort of payment. A ransom," King added.

"Usually, the individual is targeted, and the person you want payment from isn't," Stark said. This was how it usually went, but he sensed that this was no regular kidnapping. The motive wasn't money.

"Any CCTV of the parking lot across from the Red Canyon café?"

"Nothing of that part of it. It's a tiny town, and it's an old lot. One of the reasons the café is so popular is that it's the only game in town."

"Get with local and pull any CCTV of the area. Track a white car. Or the persons of interest—both Randolph and this woman. Intersections and the like. A grid—you know the drill. We'll regroup in the evening. Plane tickets and itinerary will be sent to you. We need to get Garnier on-site at that Maine beach house."

CHAPTER 25

Garnier watched from the motel-room window as Stark's sedan pulled out onto the two-lane blacktop in front of the place and drove away. He didn't lie down, didn't rest.

He tried to remote-view what he had remote-viewed while at the morgue.

He concentrated.

Nothing came.

At the autopsy table, when he touched the body, she had appeared to him. She had looked sickly and pale. She sat still as could be, the pallid skin of her face giving off an eerie glow in a room dim and shadowed. He caught a glimpse of another figure in the dark recesses in a far corner of the room. A shadow among shadows. He couldn't tell whether it was human.

Outside the window behind her, a neon sign glowed in the blue-black night.

STARL TE MO EL.

It seemed Garnier was not the only one relegated to a motel.

Yes, *sickly* was the word that came to him. Yet something else too.

Sad. Sad and lonely. Her spectral face seemed to hover in the darkness as if detached from her body.

Sad. Lonely.

And afraid.

This was not the woman who had the energy or the wherewithal to kill two men, unless she had gone into a steep decline in just the past few days.

This was someone in trouble. Someone in need of help.

He had to find her. Go to her. He had to know for himself whether she had done the terrible things she was accused of doing. He had to know for himself and not just go by CCTV footage or by King's or Stark's assessment. He needed to find out for himself, *by* himself. If it turned out that she was responsible, Garnier would call Stark, tell him where he was and where she could be found. She would not pose a physical threat to Garnier or be at risk of fleeing from him.

CHAPTER 26

"It must have been one of our hands, or a landscaper or supplier," Baxter said as he smoothed his white mustache with his thumb and pinkie.

Before going to the cabin to see Sarah, Stark had come straight here to the big house, to get Baxter's perspective on this man Francis had talked to.

Baxter and Stark sat outside at a table, in the shade of a hickory tree. The day was hot and swampy, and entirely too bright. The shade did little to alleviate either the heat or the glare, making Stark more listless than he already felt. He drank ice water from a tall glass with a sprig of mint, set before him by a thin, elderly Latina with a stoop and glistening eyes.

"You have someone in mind who looks like that?" Stark asked.

Baxter held up his hands, palms out. "It's a rather general description. I think you'd agree, being in the field you're in."

Stark did agree; the details were thin.

"Honestly, I don't know many of the people who work for me," Baxter said. "My farm manager, Leonard, oversees all hiring, personnel, and the like. He'd know better than I. But there are close to a hundred people employed here in one form or another—part-time, full-time, seasonal, salaried, and hourly. Vets, trainers, groomers, landscapers, building maintenance, barn help. Suppliers who come and go, and boarders, and riders. If I had to guess, I'd say your man was a boarder or a rider, if they were at the rail you said they were at, just down from the cabin. Probably watching horses in the paddock. There are dozens of thoroughbreds out there. Let me text Leonard."

Baxter picked his phone up off the table and texted. He took a long drink from his glass, then dabbed the sweat on his forehead with a hand-kerchief he produced from his blazer pocket. Stark had no idea how the man could endure the heat in such an outfit.

Stark drank his water and set his glass down. The ice cubes made a satisfying *clack-clack*.

"Do you have security cameras at the entrance?" Stark said.

"Of course. What's going on here? Is this something to do with your big case, the serial-killer case? What is his name?"

"It's nothing to do with that," Stark said.

"But security cameras? You must feel threatened. Or that your son is. Just your being here, their being here."

"It's to decompress, as I said. A change of scenery."

Baxter's phone pinged. Baxter glanced at it.

"Leonard will be right along," he said.

As they waited, Baxter said, "I can't help but ask, and I know you'll give the same old mum's-the-word, but are you any closer to apprehending that monster—what's he called?"

"I know who you mean," Stark said. "I don't like media monikers. And you're right, I can't talk about an ongoing investigation."

"I hope you get that cretin. Families. Children. It's all rather—ah, here he is," he said.

Leonard was tall and broad and solid. His suntanned face was spattered with darker freckles, and his red hair, buzzed close, shimmered in the sun. His green Dickies shirt was tucked neatly into a pair of Car-hartt pants. His leather boots were scuffed.

"We have several folks who work and board here who might have been the man your son spoke to," Leonard said after Stark gave him the description. His hand moved in a quick sweep to catch a fly in front of his face, squeezed, and relaxed. The dead fly fell from his grasp. "It describes a lot of middle-aged or late-middle-aged men, especially from a kid's eyes. The same way all boys from fourteen to twenty-five look the same to me now with their lanky awkwardness, noses too big for their faces, mops of unruly hair. A boy your son's age sees anyone more than twenty-five years old, and that person just registers as old. I could try to round up a few men I have in mind and ask them if they were at that fence at that time, if they spoke to your son."

"Do any of them spend time there normally?"

"You bet." He caught another fly in midair. This time when he opened his hand, the fly buzzed away. "Hell, I do. Those horses, they draw you in. I find myself pausing most days at one point or another, and I've been here going on two decades. Magnificent creatures. Spellbinding with their grace and power and athleticism. Then again, I'm a horseman, but so is just about everybody who works here."

"So, it's not unusual for someone to stop at that fence for a spell?"

"It'd be unusual if less than half a dozen people stopped during the day. Again, I can ask around, see who was there who fits the description."

Stark doubted it was necessary for Leonard to do this now, but he had taken the man's time, so he said, "I'd appreciate that."

Baxter dipped his chin at Leonard—dismissed—and Leonard walked back to his slate-gray King Cab truck and drove away.

"I hope that puts you somewhat at ease," Baxter said.

It did, partly. Sarah and Francis were way out here on the back acres, not visible from the road. It was far likelier that someone with business at the stables had been at the fence watching the horses than that Stark's father had somehow tracked them all the way out here.

———

Francis was outside playing with some sticks in the dirt at the back of the cabin. Stark wanted to speak to Sarah first, so he kept out of the boy's view and went inside.

"It wasn't my father," he said to Sarah as he came up behind her at the kitchen sink.

She turned from the pot she was scrubbing. "How can you be sure?" she said. When she didn't welcome him with a hug, he chalked it up to the wet, sudsy dish gloves she wore.

"The farm manager said people watch horses from that fence every day, and he knew a handful of men who fit the description."

"Can Francis meet these men, to be sure?" She cocked her head sideways, the way she did when her question was rhetorical.

Stark answered anyway. "It's not necessary."

"If a witness in one of your cases saw somebody do something, wouldn't you bring in a lineup of suspects?" She peeled the dishwashing gloves off her hands and draped them over the faucet, then returned her full attention to Stark.

"Witnesses are unreliable," he said.

"You don't think Francis is capable of recognizing the man he saw?" Her voice was edged with anger now.

"Of course, but he's a boy. To the young, all adults look similar—they look old."

"Dad!" Francis shouted as he burst through the door. He hugged Stark's legs, and Stark lifted him up and swung him and pulled him close, kissed his cheeks and forehead.

"My big boy!" he said and lifted him up high.

"You're back!" Francis said. "Can we go home now?"

Stark set the boy down and said, "I'm only here today and tomorrow. Then I have to get back to work."

Francis groaned and withdrew from Stark, sulking. "Mom and I could go back ourselves." He glanced at Sarah. "Can't we? I don't understand why we can't."

Stark didn't understand why Francis was so eager to go back to where he had suffered so much trauma. Perhaps it was as simple a matter as the boy's love of home being greater than the trauma he had experienced there. To him, his home was still home.

Stark glanced at Sarah, at a loss for what to tell the boy.

Sarah said nothing.

"Let's give it some time," Stark said. "After everything that happened."

"After *what* happened?" Francis said.

Stark was perplexed. "The bad stuff," he said. "With that man. At the house."

Francis gave him a quizzical look, as if he were overreacting or speaking of something Francis knew nothing about. It unsettled Stark. It frightened him.

"Come here," Sarah said to Francis, her voice soft, patient.

He stepped over to his mother. She knelt in front of him so they were eye to eye.

"I don't want to go back," she said. "I can't go back."

"But it's *home*." Francis's voice splintered, on the verge of tears.

"Wherever we are, together, is home," Sarah said.

"This isn't home," Francis said. "It's fun, but it's not home. Home is where my bed is. And all my stuffies and Dad's car in the garage and your junk journal stuff."

"I know," Sarah said. "It has a special place in all our hearts. It was our home."

"It still is." The boy's voice caught.

"I want you to have all the time you need to adjust," Sarah said. She touched Francis's cheek with the back of her hand. "It's just, I can't—"

Francis was crying now. Silently. Tears streaked his cheeks.

"Let's take a break, okay?" Stark said. "We don't have to decide anything this minute."

"It's decided," Sarah said, and stood up. She folded her arms across her chest. "It was decided *for* us. Let me get you some breakfast, Francis. You haven't eaten yet, and it's late."

Sarah shook Froot Loops into a bowl and splashed milk over it, then went to the bedroom to get dressed.

Stark sat across the table as Francis pushed the cereal around in his bowl with his spoon.

"I heard you met someone while you were watching the horses," Stark said, trying to strike an offhand, casual tone.

Francis scooped a bite of cereal, slurping and wiping the dribble of milk off his chin.

Stark repeated himself.

Francis took a bite of cereal and gave him a quizzical look.

"A man at the fence," Stark explained.

"The man you told me about," Sarah said as she came back in the room, pulling her hair back in a ponytail and catching it in a hair band. "The strange man."

"Oh yeah," Francis said. "He wasn't strange."

This was a different take from what Sarah had told Stark.

"He sounded strange. To me," Sarah said, her voice tight, defensive. "What he said to you was strange."

"What did he say?" Francis said.

"Don't you remember?" Sarah prodded. "About whom you look like."

"He didn't say I looked like anyone."

"Yes, he did," Sarah said. "You told me he did."

"No, I didn't."

"You did. You said he said you looked like his own son."

"That's not what he said. He said I reminded him of his son when he was my age. He never said I looked like him."

"Well, it's the same thing," Sarah said. "He was insinuating it. Sending a message."

This was not the same as saying Francis looked like his son. This was a much more general statement. Francis might have reminded the man of his son for any number of reasons. Just a perceived love of horses if Francis was watching the thoroughbreds. Or maybe the color or style of his hair. Or just being a young boy in general—it might have brought up feelings of nostalgia. It was an innocuous statement any older man might say to a young child. Still, Stark wanted to follow up on it some to satisfy himself there was no threat, that it was not his father.

"Did he say if he worked here, for the farm?"

"No." Francis finished his cereal and stirred the remaining milk with his spoon.

"Did he say he was family?"

"Why would he say he was family?"

"Your mom mentioned—"

"He didn't say that."

"No?" Stark said. He was in part relieved to hear this but confused too. Sarah had just told him the man had said he was family. Now Francis was refuting that.

"He said I reminded him of his own boy so much we could be family."

Could be family. That wasn't the same.

"And where did the man go? Was he driving a car?"

"I don't know. He disappeared."

"What do you mean?"

Stark could feel Sarah watching him, hanging on each word.

"I was feeding the horses," Francis said, "and the man stopped saying anything. And then when I went to go inside, he wasn't there anymore. I wasn't paying attention. He was just some man. I want to go back to our real home."

Stark couldn't fault Sarah for extrapolating from what Francis had said. For being on edge and on guard. He appreciated it, encouraged it, even if it was a source of stress for her. Both she and Stark were on edge after what Q had done and after Stark's father showed up at the house. And she had a point. His father might say that very thing. It might have been him. Or it might not.

"Had you seen him around before?" Stark said.

"I don't think so," Francis said. He picked up his cereal bowl and tilted it to slurp the milk.

"Don't do that," Sarah said too late.

"Will you tell me and your mom if you do?" Stark said.

"Is he a bad man? Is he a killer?"

"No, sweetie," Sarah said. "God, no." She picked up the bowl off the table and set it in the sink.

"Who is he? What did he do?" Francis said.

"He's no one," Stark said. "We thought maybe he was, but I don't know."

"Someone bad," Francis said. "Is there a bad man out there who wants to hurt me?"

Stark expected Francis to complete his thought with something along the lines of *like the man at the house the other night*, but he didn't.

"Forget we said anything," Sarah said. "Can you do that?"

"Okay," Francis said. "I won't think about it anymore."

It seemed to Stark the boy was being literal. He would stop thinking about it in that instant and not think of it again, wipe it so resolutely from his mind that it was as if it had never happened at all.

———

In the late afternoon, as Stark drove out of the estate for the airport, he saw a man standing under the poplars across the road from the horse farm's gate. He was bald and smoking a cigarette and seemed to be watching the entrance.

For a moment, Stark thought it was his father.

He drove slowly past the man and took a long, hard look at him.

It was not his father. There was no mistake. It was a man who could have been his father but wasn't.

Stark pulled over and got out of the car and approached the man.

"Nice day," the man said as he flicked his cigarette butt to the gravel and ground it out with the heel of his boot.

He looked across the road, toward the farm. Stark looked in the same direction.

"Waiting on someone?" Stark said.

"Coworker. She gives me a ride home from work. The farm's a no-smoking premises, so I try to sneak one in really quick. She won't let me smoke in her car either."

"You work on the farm?"

"Fifteen years."

The man was too young to be Stark's father. He was not even Stark's age, but to a boy, he'd still have been an old man.

He wasn't wearing a ball cap, but Stark supposed he could have been wearing one earlier, while working in the sun.

"You ever watch the horses by the back paddock?" Stark said.

"Time to time. Why?" The man gave him an inquisitive look, and Stark realized that he himself was the one acting suspicious.

"No reason. My son likes to watch them. We're staying in the cabin."

"Oh, yeah. Okay. I've seen your son around."

"Did you see him yesterday?"

"No. I was working with a rider, in the arena. Here she is."

A pickup truck pulled out of the farm entrance and swung up to them.

Stark watched as the man got in and the truck drove away.

CHAPTER 27

"They're safe, for now," S says. She holds her phone up for Randolph to see his wife and daughter and granddaughters on a live video stream.

"Safe?" Randolph says, his voice strained. "You've abducted them. Taken them to who knows where. Tormented them. Done something to paralyze them. What? What have you done?"

"It's reversible. Within a certain period of time. I am going to tell you what you need to do to free your family, and you either do it or not. The choice is yours."

"How do I know you're telling the truth?"

S leans toward Randolph's face, lifts his chin to look her in the eye. He can't move his head or neck, but he shifts his eyes away from hers.

"You don't know," S says, and stands up straight. "You have to trust that I am."

"Trust someone who drugged and abducted my family and me."

"As I said, the choice is yours."

"Why should I believe you?"

"Why should *I* believe *you*?" S says, biting the words. "You are a proven liar. I'm supposed to believe that you never imagined your discoveries could be used in the way they're being used." She watches his eyes and waits for the reply to tell her she is correct.

And it comes.

He blinks.

"I didn't know," he says. "I still don't. Not the specifics. I admit, I suspected."

"They paid you more than your honorarium, didn't they?"

Randolph admits that they did.

"Which explains the beach house."

"Yes."

"And you knew they were going to use your advances for their cause."

"I didn't know. But I also knew it wasn't impossible if they elected to pursue it."

"And now I put the question to you: Will you elect to do what I ask, and spare your family and society? Or will you not?"

CHAPTER 28

The beach house was a grand old place, with its widow's walk and its wraparound porch and back patio facing the Atlantic. The cedar roof shakes had gone pewter with weathering from the ceaseless winds, unsparing sun, and long, brutal Maine winters.

The field leading up to it reminded Stark of the painting by Wyeth, of the woman in the field. He had read somewhere that the woman was a neighbor of Andrew Wyeth's; she had been paralyzed from the waist down. It added an entirely new dimension to the painting, knowing this. Knowing that the woman who modeled for it might not be able to reach the house herself, or that it might take hours of dragging herself to get there.

King and Stark and Garnier entered the house. It was quiet inside, but they could hear the squawk of gulls outside, hovering on the wind past the plate-glass windows that took in the view of the beach. The tide must have been at its peak, for the waves were no more than fifty feet from the house—so close the mist from their crashing blurred the patio windows to make an impressionist scene of the outdoors.

The kitchen island was a massive slab of quartz. The ceilings had to be twelve feet high. The cabinets were a pristine white, the floors a blond hardwood. It was a gorgeous kitchen, a chef's kitchen. Yet it had a smell—of the sugar water that had been left to burn on the stove.

"There was no sign of a struggle," Stark said.

"None," King affirmed.

Garnier walked around the perimeter of the open-concept living room off the kitchen, looking at photographs of the family, and the artwork and small sculptures, the vast built-in bookcases shelved with hardcover volumes in the fields of chemistry and biology.

"Where are the twins' bedrooms?" he said.

———

There was only one bedroom for the twins.

King had expected there to be two and for them to be large. But there was just the one and it was modest though tasteful. The walls were painted a light warm peach color, with white curtains that fluttered at the windows, which were cracked open a bit. The twin beds were parallel, each covered with a white comforter and adorned with stuffed animals and large pillows like marshmallows.

Garnier sat on the edge of a bed. He picked up a stuffed lion and shut his eyes. He became very calm.

King looked on, not knowing what to make of this spectacle.

Garnier began to rock gently in place. He made no sound. The stuffed lion fell from his grip to the floor.

"I need something else," he said, and stood up.

"Nothing?" Stark said.

"Not even blackness."

Garnier looked around the room and walked out into the hall and back into the kitchen.

He set his hand on the counter. "Ah, damn!" he said.

"What?" Stark said.

Garnier picked his hand up from the island. A dot of blood marked the center of his palm.

"What is that?" King said.

Hanging from Garnier's palm was a broken piece of a hypodermic needle, perhaps an inch long.

Garnier stiffened, and his eyes rolled up.

King stood back in surprise.

Garnier closed his hand around the needle. Blood dripped onto the island as he swayed in place. King cringed at the sight of yellow mucus leaking from his ear.

"I see them," Garnier said. "Four of them. In chairs. The twins. Mother and grandmother. They seem immobile. But they are not bound. It's as if they have been paralyzed."

"Are they alive?" Stark said.

"They are. The grandmother is speaking. She can't move, but it seems she can speak."

King edged closer to Garnier. She didn't know whether what he was saying was true for anyone but himself, but she felt that he believed what he was seeing and what he was conveying. It was beyond anything she had experienced.

"Describe the surroundings," Stark said. "Who is she speaking to?"

"It's hard to see. There's a bright light shining on them, like an interrogator's light. Someone is standing behind it."

Garnier recoiled. "The light is shining right at me now. I—"

His cell phone rang.

He broke from his trance, put the phone on speaker.

"Hello," he said.

"Hello, X. I've been waiting for you. We all have. Waiting and watching. I see your friends are with you."

"V," Garnier said. "V. Listen to me. This isn't who you are. Let them go."

"It is who I am. Free. No longer subject to the program's oppression and exploitation."

"Hurting people," Garnier said. "Kids and women. *This* is you?"

"They are not hurt."

"Not physically, perhaps. But you've hurt them. Injured their very being."

"They'll recover, just as we must. I wouldn't do this if I didn't have to. For others."

"For whom?" Garnier said.

"Society."

"That's a bit broad—"

"This is Agent Stark," Stark said.

"I know," V said. "I can see you there. King too. Standing around the island, with X's hand bleeding. It took getting jabbed by a needle to prompt you to view me. See how you are weakening, my friend."

King felt disbelief and awe. This person on the phone, this V, saw them here. Somehow. It shook her, left her feeling unmoored. She shivered, then gathered herself.

"I am not a friend," Garnier said. "We have never been friends. Let them go."

"I can't do that until other criteria are met."

"What criteria?" Stark said.

"This doesn't involve you," V said. "It involves X. And the rest of us."

"Rest of *who*?" King said.

"Us. The six of us. Led by Q."

"Q is out of circulation," Stark said.

V laughed. "And you know this how?"

"I turned him over."

"Turned him over to whom?"

Stark's face tightened.

"The program," he said.

"*Who* in the program?"

Stark didn't answer. He didn't know; it was clear to King. He didn't know who he had turned Q over to on the side of the road. Regret lined his face.

"You don't even know who it was. You acted like a dog, serving your superior, afraid to push back lest it cost you a paycheck. Just dropped a murderer off on the side of the road to someone you never met before, because you did as you were told. Just taking orders, isn't that so?"

Stark didn't reply. His face turned pink, and King didn't know whether it was from anger or embarrassment, or both.

"You released him to someone who was also just following orders," V said. "A peon. Someone no match for Q. Someone now dead. Whoever you thought Q was, whatever you thought of him, as just another serial killer with a warped mind, you had him wrong. He is a warrior of truth, and he will fight for it."

"Where are you?" Stark said. "Release them and tell us where you are so we can end this safely. For everyone."

"There is only one way to end it: for those responsible to be reprogrammed or . . . held accountable. Randolph must publicly denounce his part. We tried to convince the others to do likewise."

"What others?" Stark said.

"Phyllis and Friede."

"What did they do?" Garnier said. "Their research was for the good and had hardly anything to do with the other."

"Dig deeper and you will see the connection."

The call ended.

Garnier held his hand up for Stark and King to remain still so he could focus.

He narrowed his eyes but did not close them, as if trying to see something in the distance.

Then he blinked and came back.

He pulled the needle from his palm and ran the faucet over the puncture as he squeezed blood out.

"I saw something," he said. His voice was calm, eyes glassy. "Just as he swung the light back down on his hostages."

King could hardly grasp what was happening.

"What?" Stark said.

"Out a window, in the room behind him. I saw a truck go by. Or more of a van, or a work truck. Not a pickup. White. With a yellow sun on the side."

"Any windows?" King said.

"No windows."

"A yellow sun," King said. "What can that mean?"

"A bakery," Stark said. "Or a flower shop. Or a farm. Or a solar company. Or a rehab. Check them all out. Get someone on it. For the entire New England region. Have AI run an entire scraping of any and all entities that have a sun on their logo. You"—Stark looked at Garnier—"find a piece of paper here, a pen or pencil. Draw it. Draw the sun you saw. Is it just a ball? Is it yellow, or more orange? Does it have rays, and if so, are they symmetrical, like on the New Mexico flag? Is it a photographic image, or more of a cartoon? Draw it the best you can. Then write a description."

Garnier ransacked the kitchen drawers until he found a pencil and notepad and drew what he had viewed. He handed it to Stark.

"Good," Stark said. He handed the drawing and description to King. "Have 'em run this. Now. All New England."

CHAPTER 29

Garnier backed away from his motel window and shut the curtain. He had seen something else when he tried to remote-view.

He saw S again.

Again, she was in a room at the Starlite Motel. She seemed sicker than ever, in desperate need of help.

He called for an taxi, which arrived ten minutes later.

As he slid into the back seat, he said, "Airport."

CHAPTER 30

Agent King knocked at the door of the 1980s suburban raised ranch and was soon greeted by a woman in a rumpled gray sweat suit with a coffee stain on the front.

Her black hair was unkempt and greasy, and she was without makeup. Her pink eyes and wet nose made her look as if she might be suffering from a bad cold, but it was not that, King knew. It was grief. King knew something of this herself. Her father had passed away six months and eight days ago. A sudden stroke—here and gone.

"Mrs. Cutter?" King asked, though she knew it must be the wife of the dead man.

The woman offered a nearly imperceptible nod. "Beverly," she said, her voice frail.

"I am sorry for your loss," King said.

Beverly Cutter made a sound in her throat and led King up the stairs to a living room. Her bare feet were small and pink.

Mrs. Cutter didn't offer King anything to drink or eat, as many individuals being interviewed tended to do. King was relieved. It was not a necessary gesture, and King liked to focus on things that were necessary.

On the beige walls hung pictures of the woman with her husband and what had to be their daughter, in various stages of their lives together.

King sat on the faux-leather couch, and the woman sat opposite her in a matching recliner.

"I have everything you requested right here," the woman said, and reached out to touch a stack of folders on the coffee table between them.

King thanked her.

"He printed everything out," Mrs. Cutter said.

"We'll need his laptop too," King said.

"He used a desktop."

"That's fine. We'll have someone come get it. We'll need it. There might be information on there about who hired him for this work. Do you have *any* idea?"

"I don't have a description, but I know it was a woman," Mrs. Cutter said. She wiped her nose with a tissue and tucked the tissue into the cuff of her sweatshirt sleeve.

"How do you know?" King said.

"He said as much. Her name was Kate."

This surprised King. The name had to be fake. It wasn't much to go on, but at least it narrowed the possibilities to 51 percent of the population.

"Did you ever hear him speak to her? Ever hear her voice?"

"I stayed out of it. His acting. He was a good actor. But he never got that lucky break, you know? So much of it is luck and timing and who you know and . . . He was happy to get the work. He told me he'd given up believing his break would ever come, but I think there was always a glimmer of hope in him. We lived in Los Angeles for a decade when we were younger. It was something, to be a part of all that, even if it was only at the edges. It's a cruel business in the end, but what business isn't, I suppose? Business is business."

"I see." King felt for the woman and for her dead husband. They seemed to have been content in their lives—something few people ever managed. King herself knew the disappointment of dreams never realized.

"I can say he was excited about this venture. He said it would pay well. He said it was unusual. And in many ways, it was."

"How so?"

"Well. It troubled me a bit, I must admit. It was a role, he said—two roles, actually, like theater, because it was live, except that he would play to a small, limited audience. He had two roles. He couldn't say where he was to do it, what the roles were, or who the audience was. As part of taking the work, he was not allowed to tell anyone—not even me—anything about it. It seemed . . . honestly, it seemed kind of bizarre, shady even. I was against it. To me, it smacked of a scam by someone pretending to be wealthy."

"Why wealthy?" King leaned forward on the couch, taking notes on her tablet.

"The money was a lot. For us, anyway. That's why I finally said he should do it. Money." Beverly looked down at her hands folded in her lap. "I should never have been tempted by that carrot."

"How much money?"

"Ten thousand dollars. They gave him five up front. In cash." She rubbed her hands, picked at the cuticle of a thumb.

"Cash?" King said.

"That troubled me too. When he told me they paid in cash, I told him he had to give it back and tell them thanks but no. Then he showed it to me, the cash. I was excited and confused and worried at the same time. But I relented. And the first role he played, he told me it went well. It was fun. It was easy. He worked hard on the role. Took an entire week off his day job as a property inspector to nail his lines and his marks. Still, five thousand dollars was a lot for forty hours of rehearsing. Then he told me it was for someone wealthy, and it was all for some sort of secret prank this wealthy person was playing. He said he wasn't allowed to say more and didn't know much more. But it was good money and harmless."

"Did you ever hear him rehearse?"

Beverly shook her head. "He rehearsed in the spare room upstairs so he could focus."

"How did he come to learn of this work?"

"An agent called him, said a director had seen his work and wondered if he was still acting. He tried to keep his enthusiasm in check, but I could see it thrilled him."

"Do you know the agent's name?"

"I don't."

"This agent just called out of the blue?" King didn't know anything about the industry, but it seemed a bit too fortuitous.

"It happened every once in a while, very rarely. But usually, it was for doing a local car dealership's voice-over, or maybe work for a PBS fundraiser. Something low-key like that, which he was glad to do."

"Did this agent call your husband's cell?"

"Yes."

"When?"

She thought. "Somewhere around the tenth, in July? We were in Boston that week when he got the call."

"We can check his cell-phone log, see the number it came from."

"Oh, that's good. You think . . ." She blew her nose into another tissue she plucked from a box beside her. "This wasn't an accident."

"We're not sure. But we want to be sure. Either way. Whoever called, their number will be found. It will be a start."

"Thank you."

"Do you know the password for your husband's desktop?" King said.

"There isn't one. It's too old."

King looked at the stack of folders.

"You can help yourself to them," the woman said. "Take them with you if you need, and his computer too. It's there on the desk by the fireplace. If you don't mind, I think I need to lie down for a bit."

Not waiting for a reply, the grieving widow shuffled down the hallway, went into a room, and shut the door behind her.

King picked up the top folder. It was heavy. In it were a dozen headshots taken over the past thirty years—a new group of shots every two or three years. The man aging before her. Nothing interesting there. She set them aside. There were letters, then email exchanges printed out, soliciting representation from various agents and managers. All the exchanges ended with congenial enough rejections of representation, but rejections, nonetheless.

There were a few contracts from the 1990s, when he did pick up work for characters in a few TV shows, and some clippings from magazines such as *People* and *US* and *Entertainment Weekly*, in which his name was mentioned. One article included a photograph of him with other cast members, from a TV show King had never heard of but that apparently was successful for two seasons. He was standing with a handful of other cast members, in the back, smiling. He had a tremendous smile. He was a handsome man. Even here, twenty-five years ago, there was a noticeable likeness to Director Valken. In this photo, someone had circled him in red marker. King wondered if it was he who had circled himself, or his wife, or perhaps a friend or a manager.

King examined several folders that contained much of the same material from over the years.

She took them in chronological order, from the early 1990s to present day, each folder getting progressively slimmer until the one marked *2020*, which had printouts of two royalty checks, for $12.79 and $17.49.

At the desk, King inspected papers left out around the computer and in the drawer. There was nothing of note.

She searched the desktop. Forensics would come in after her and take it with them and do a thorough dive for deleted files, images, and documents and the like.

King discovered nothing in her brief search, except for one item that let her know this was indeed the man who had played the role of Director Valken. It was a script. Two pages.

VALKEN *(holding out hand to shake)*
Good to meet you. I'm Director Valken . . .

When she finished reading the script, King was unsure whether she should knock on the door the widow had disappeared behind, or just leave without notice.

As if hearing King's thoughts, Beverly Cutter stepped out into the hall.

"I hope this was some help," she said, entering the room.

"There will be other investigators, from forensics, coming to take his desktop and files and anything else at all connected to this role he played. Anything you can think of."

"Would they want his jacket?" the woman said. "He got a very nice suit to wear for the first role, and he came home with it on. It fit him impeccably. He was more excited about it than the money, I think."

King kept her face neutral, squelching the impulse to smile.

"Yes, please bring the suit out. Have it ready for them. Is it on a hanger?"

"Oh, yes."

"Carry it by the hanger and hang it on the door."

A knock came.

"That will be them now," King said.

When the forensics team of four entered, King directed leader Hakeem Panden to the computer, the files, and the suit. "I want this suit addressed right away. It looks tailored. Track down where. Find out."

Her phone buzzed. An encrypted email had arrived. Subject: VAN SEARCH.

She read the email and rang Stark and Garnier on a group call.

Garnier's phone went to voicemail.

"I just got photos in an email," she said. "I think we've got our van. A solar company based in Concord, New Hampshire. They have a fleet of about twenty vans, in a region that covers some two hundred square miles, going east toward Portsmouth and west toward Keene."

"Bring Garnier in on this."

"I tried to get him on the call. It went to voicemail."

She got off the call with Stark and tried Garnier's phone again. And again.

No answer. She texted. Waited ten minutes. Got no reply.

In fact, the text wasn't even read, by the looks of it.

Where the hell was he?

CHAPTER 31

The plane touched down with a jolt that woke Garnier. He had slept fitfully the entire way and was now awake, unrested, and disoriented.

With no checked baggage, he blew past the carousels and made straight for the car rental agency.

An hour later, he was just outside the town he had remote-viewed, the Starlite Motel coming up on the right.

Garnier drove the dark street of the quiet town, boxed in by an eighteen-wheeler in front of him and another behind him, its headlights turning the interior of his rental car bright as day. Every third shop window was either boarded up or soaped with STOREWIDE CLEARANCE!!! or CLOSEOUT BLOWOUT! FOR LEASE.

The shops that still seemed to be in business were dark for the night. The Café Sunrise. Bronze Age Tanning Salon. A massage therapist.

He passed a post office and a real estate brokerage.

He pulled into the Starlite's parking lot and swung the car into the row of parking spaces in front of the row of rooms. To the left, down at the end, a sign that read OFFICE rocked in the breeze. He didn't know the room number, but this was the place. There was no mistaking the pink-and-green neon sign proclaiming the *STARL TE MO EL.*

He got out and walked along the walkway in front of the rooms. The place was poorly lit with one low-watt yellowish floodlight at either end of the row of rooms. He tried to assess the angle from which he had remote-viewed the motel sign out front. He could rule out several of the rooms straightaway, starting with the two at the ends. The perspective wouldn't be correct. It had to be one of the middle five rooms, but he couldn't know which of the five. He stood in front of each window, hoping no one would see him or his silhouette outside. The first and last of the five remaining rooms seemed unlikely too. He crouched for a different point of view, to approximate her sitting in a chair. He decided the room she was in had to be either 115 or 116. He scrutinized the sign from outside each window.

He backed up and looked at one window. Then the other.

A metallic *click* startled him. He looked left to see a man coming out of a room three doors down—119. The man was barefoot and his wild heap of white hair disheveled. He wore khaki shorts and a tropical-print shirt of a vibrant yellow and orange. The shirt was unbuttoned to reveal his ample, pale gut. He stretched backward, pressing his fists into his lower back as he belched.

He seemed to sense he was being watched and turned and gawped at Garnier. He offered a nod of acknowledgment, as if unsurprised to see a stranger standing out in front of the rooms after midnight.

He scratched behind his knee, inspected his fingernails, then grinned and went back inside.

Garnier looked at the sign again.

Room 115—it had to be.

The curtains inside the window were parted slightly.

Garnier cupped his hands around his eyes and tried to peer in.

"What are you doing?" a voice bellowed.

Garnier's heart kicked, and he felt his face warm.

He stepped back from the window to see a man—fifties or so, tall and bony—hitching toward him with a severe limp. His face was gone to leather from sun abuse. "What the hell?"

The man who had come outside earlier, Hawaiian-shirt guy, stepped out of room 119 again and stared at Garnier. His shirt was buttoned now.

Garnier stepped in front of the door to 115.

"Checking on a friend," he said.

"That right?" the man said. His ribbed white V-neck T-shirt was untucked, with a yellow stain dead center of his chest. The stain appeared to be mustard. His corduroy pants hung precariously from his bony hips and looked in danger of falling down. He wasn't just skinny, Garnier saw, but sinewy, with muscles like knotted rope. Even in the low light, the man's eyes were an alarming bright blue.

"Checking on a friend? At twelve thirty in the morning. What friend?" the man said. His voice was ragged and reedy, the voice of a man who had smoked filterless cigarettes since he was thirteen.

"She didn't answer my knock," Garnier said. "But she told me to meet her here."

"She. That right?" The man rested his hands on his hip bones, in a gunslinger's stance. "What kind of friend?"

"An *old* friend."

"Knock again. It's late; maybe she fell asleep. We'll see if she's expecting you. Your *friend*."

Garnier had no choice now but to knock on the door to 115.

He rapped on the door, and it opened so fast it startled him. When he saw who it was, he was startled all the more.

"I expected you earlier," the woman said.

"You know this man?" Bony Man said to her.

"From another life."

Bony Man looked confused. Then, without a word, he retreated toward the office at a fast clip, looking back once and continuing even faster.

"Come in," she said.

Garnier entered room 115 and felt a beesting at his neck. In the time it took him to swat at it, the syringe was sunk deep into his spine, and his hand was already heavy and numb as an anvil.

As he sank into darkness, he heard a voice say again, "I'm sorry." But he couldn't tell if it was his own voice or that of a woman he thought he knew.

S.

CHAPTER 32

Garnier woke.

The pain in his neck was sharp and hot, as if the tip of an ice pick taken straight from a forge were being pushed in between the vertebrae.

He squeezed his eyes tight against the pain, gritted his teeth.

The back of his skull felt strange now—numb and prickly.

When he tried to touch the back of his head with his hand, he couldn't.

He couldn't move. He could feel his hands but couldn't get them to do what he needed them to do.

"Don't fret," a voice behind him said.

Garnier knew the voice.

Q.

What was he doing here? How did he get here? Had he escaped from the program *again*?

Garnier tried to turn to the voice, but he couldn't move. Why not? He could feel himself, feel his body, his hands resting on the arms of the chair, feel the ropes that bound him, digging into his wrists and ankles.

He tried again to move but couldn't. Willed himself, to no avail. He sat there, defenseless. Terrified.

"We have to talk," Q said. The voice was at his ear now, whispering. Garnier could feel hot breath on his skin.

"Where is she?" Garnier said. "Where is S? What did you do to her?"

"She's nearby, doing her part."

"What did you trick her into doing for you?"

"Tsk tsk. *Trick?* What do you take me for? I didn't trick her into anything. She's her own individual who makes her own choices. She chooses well, I must admit."

"Where am I?" Garnier said.

"Where we are is hardly important. What and how we are *is*."

"What have you done to me?"

"Nothing that cannot be reversed with your cooperation."

"Reverse it now," Garnier said.

"I would, but I don't trust you."

"*You* don't trust *me*?" Garnier said.

"In general, I do. Just not at this particular moment. You're too worked up and you seem to be under the wrong impression about me."

"You killed families. In cold blood. *Executed children*."

"You misunderstand completely. But I'll rectify that."

"I know what you did. Nothing you say will change that. And Stark and I caught you in the act with his wife and son. If we hadn't stopped you, they'd be dead too."

"You are mistaken. You saw what you wanted to see—you and your friend both."

Stark was not a friend. Garnier didn't have any friends, just as Q didn't.

"You needed to be stopped," Garnier said. "Even you know that. Even you know that any ordinary person, a person not twisted by the program, would want to stop you. That what you were doing was wrong."

"What was I doing?" Q said. "You keep saying I was killing families."

"I'm not *saying* it. You did, and that is fact."

"You sure about that?"

"As sure as I am about anything."

"As sure as you once were that what we did for the program was just and righteous? That we had once been a part of real families who had somehow . . . what? Sacrificed us so the program could make use of us for some greater cause?"

Garnier didn't answer. He had begun to question all of that: whether he was ever from a family who willingly gave him up; whether what he did for the program was just, was for the greater good. But one thing had nothing to do with the other. He was not going to let Q plant seeds of doubt in his mind. Doubt was the poison that corroded reason. Nor would he let Q create some false equivalency between Garnier's own part in the program, and the murder of families.

"I know," Q said. "Just because you once believed in a reality concocted entirely for us doesn't mean that what I am telling you now is true. But it is. Why else would I lure you here to see me?"

"To kill me."

Q laughed with such sudden violence it startled Garnier.

"I couldn't kill you. We are one and the same. To kill you is to kill myself."

"We are not the same," Garnier said.

"You are my family. You are here in this chair for your own good, to protect yourself from yourself, and to protect me from you."

"Protect *you* from *me*? What do you think I'd do to you?"

"I don't want to find out. But what I need from you now is to listen to me."

Garnier didn't want to hear the delusional blather of this man he had known since they were children, listen to insane justifications for what he had done.

"I listen, and then what?" Garnier said. "You shoot me in the back of the head like you did the others?"

"I reverse your paralysis and I let you go."

"You'll just *let me go*?"

"Correct."

Garnier didn't believe him. There was no reason to. He knew he was a dead man.

"And why would you let me go?" he said. "Now that I know you're loose again, you don't think I'd tell Stark? You don't think he'd come after you? Or I would come after you with him?"

"You won't tell him or come after me—not after what I have to tell you," Q said. "And by the way, what makes you think I *escaped* from the program?"

"You're here now, aren't you?"

"I didn't escape from anyone or anything, because there was never anyone or anything for me to escape from."

"You make no sense," Garnier said.

"I will after you listen to what I came here to tell you. I haven't brought you here for anything except to have you listen. I already know what I need to know. But you don't yet know what you need to know. I am here of my own volition."

"Stark surrendered you to the program."

"And how would he know it was the program he released me back to? He just handed me over to someone he's never seen before in his life."

"Agent Franklin directed him to do it. Franklin arranged—"

"Ah yes. Agent Franklin. How is retirement treating him?"

Q grinned.

Garnier tried to work it out. What did Q know about Franklin? Did he know he was dead? Had Q remote-viewed Franklin's death? Or had something to do with it? The truth was, Garnier had no idea who Stark had handed Q over to. Perhaps it wasn't the program at all, and Franklin had been duped into thinking it was. Or Q had escaped the person Stark turned him over to. Whatever the situation, Q was not in his right mind. Garnier needed to navigate carefully, needed to give Q what he needed.

"Did Stark release you back to the program or not?" Garnier asked.

Q paced in front of him, agitated, rubbing his temples with his pinkies.

Q ignored the question. "He didn't even ask the man he handed me off to who he was or who he worked for. Just dumped me off like cargo. Let me go to an old friend of mine, and of yours too."

Garnier had no idea who this friend could be, but he had to be from the program. Garnier knew no one outside it besides Stark and King.

"Dr. Romeau," Garnier said.

CHAPTER 33

As Stark left the J. Edgar Hoover Building, he called Garnier.

He got voicemail.

"Get back to me ASAP."

Walking toward his car in the parking garage, he saw him.

His father.

He was leaning against the front of Stark's car, arms folded, waiting.

He ran a palm over his bald, tanned head.

Stark advanced on him until he stood close, in his face.

"You need to stop," he said. "I want nothing to do with you. *We* want nothing to do with you." He brushed past and grabbed the door handle.

"Your son reminds me of you," the old man said, still leaning against the grille. Not even looking at Stark.

Stark let go of the door handle. Came around and faced his father again. Closer.

"Don't talk about him."

His father lit a cigarette with a brass Zippo and squinted through the smoke at Stark.

"I bring back bad memories," the old man said. "I get that. And you fear those memories."

"No," Stark said. "I despise them. What you did. What you made me do. You make me sick. Having me, a boy, your own son, *help* you. I was eight years old."

"We all need help at times. Me, you, everyone," his father said. He took a long drag on his cigarette and blew a chain of smoke rings above his head. "I know how old you were. And I felt for you as deeply then as you feel for your own son now. I still feel for you as deeply. Perhaps more."

His father disgusted him—him of all people, daring to speak of parental love.

"I want to help you," his father said. "Just as I always have. The truth is important to know."

"I don't want to hear your rationale. Justifications for what you did."

"It makes sense that you don't want to know. But you need to know. After what I sacrificed, you at least owe it to me to hear the truth."

Stark was seething, hot anger burning in him. *Sacrificed.* His father should still be in prison for what he did to Stark's mother and to Stark. Twenty years was no sacrifice for what he'd done. "Leave us alone, or I'll—"

"You'll what?" his father said. "What will you do?"

Stark stared at his father. "You don't want to know."

"I do know. Which is why you need to hear me out, before it's too late."

"For you, it's already too late," Stark growled. "If I or Francis or Sarah see you again, you'll get what you deserve."

"I want you to think on something," his father said, and stood up straight and tall. "Ask yourself, whatever happened to the hammer you used to pound those nails into the decking that day?"

With that, his father got into his car and drove off.

The hammer, Stark thought. What had the old man meant? What was he insinuating? A memory started to rise in the back of his mind. Himself, holding the hammer. His mother . . .

His phone rang. It was King.

"You were right," she said by way of greeting. "The suit was bespoke—made by a tailor in Boston." Stark appreciated the way King skipped the pleasantries and got straight to business. "Off Newbury Street," she continued. "I have an agent out of Boston going in to interview the tailor and saleswoman in person, but I spoke to the tailor, a Joan Winthrop. She made the suit. She did not meet the customer. This was unusual. But she was told the suit was to be a gift. A woman brought in the man's measurements herself. The tailor balked at first until it was agreed if the suit didn't fit well, she could not be held accountable since she was not the one to take the measurements. She remembered that the woman was slender and wore sunglasses inside the shop. I sent her a photo of S. She said it wasn't her. She got a signature on the receipt forensics is going to get, but she also remembered the interaction because the woman paid cash."

"I didn't expect it would be S," Stark said.

"Nor did I. But there's another woman who is part of this so-called six, isn't there?"

"*Two* others. And it doesn't mean that whoever arranged for the suit knew anything about any other plan—knew why the suit was to be worn, knew any of it. I think this is how they operate: in silos. No one knows anything about anyone else's role. It allows for plausible deniability. Ultimate secrecy. It allows for a woman, tasked with getting a suit made, to know nothing more than the subject's measurements. Interrogate her, torture her—it doesn't matter; she knows nothing else. No harm done."

"We need a description of these other two women. Other than S."

"They go by *K* and *L*, I believe," Stark said.

He texted Garnier: *Who are the other two women of the Six, besides S?*

He waited and got no indication the text had been read.

He texted Garnier again: *CALL ME ASAP*, then spoke to King, "We need to go to his motel. Something's not right."

CHAPTER 34

Q stood in front of Garnier, hands clasped behind his back.

"Dr. Romeau," Garnier said again. "That's who Stark handed you off to?"

"No, one of his lackeys in the east, a proxy for him. He didn't dare get entangled in such real matters. But it was he who arranged it."

Romeau headed the program's Intensive Viewing Initiative. He created and conducted the initiative's rigorous experiments played out by Q and Garnier. He was their Mentor and trainer, and their idol. He had worked with Q and Garnier since the two were perhaps four years old. He had impressed upon the boys that they were gifted, touched by wonder, and he reminded them of this routinely. He told them that with their gifts came an obligation to sharpen their native talents. He marveled them, yet he pushed them hard.

Romeau put the boys in rooms in separate buildings and had them try to remote-view a location after giving each the same stimulus—a foreign coin whose origin and metal seemed mysterious; a stone carving of a mythological creature that fit in the palm of the hand; a knife with a long, curved blade. From this, the boys were to summon a location or a person, or both, associated with the object, the stimulus. Early on, they could not do it. "Let it come to you," Romeau would say. "You are it and it is you. Do not fight it or force it." Garnier tried. He wanted to please Romeau. And soon he could see these locations and describe them and the people in them. Without knowing that he was seeing a target two continents away, Garnier would describe it. "I see men in ties—old men. White hair. Beards. Glasses. Looking at computers. They're wearing white jackets with a patch on them."

It wasn't until he was in his late teens that Garnier began to understand what he viewed and described: military sites and research laboratories. Missile silos. Arms-manufacturing plants. Secret underground R and D facilities. Bomb test sites. Submarines. Drones.

Now he wondered, who were these people he had viewed? What were these places *really*?

Dr. Romeau gave meaning to what they were viewing. When Garnier described three old white-haired men in lab coats peering through microscopes and taking notes on laptops, using syringes to inject rabbits and chimpanzees, Romeau said Garnier was seeing experiments for chemical warfare, conducted by foreign scientists.

Garnier wondered if this was true. Dr. Romeau could have been lying to him. For all Garnier knew, those men in lab coats might have been searching for a skin-safe cosmetic or working on a vaccine for some virus. He had relied entirely on Romeau for the facts.

"Let me tell you what you are," Q said. He pulled up a chair and sat facing Garnier.

He was not as gaunt as he had been a few weeks ago at Stark's home. Not as washed out. Now there was color to his face, a brightness in his eyes. His muscles had tone. It surprised Garnier. When last they met, Q had looked like a man beyond recovery, ravaged by a physical disease and its psychological toll.

"What I did," Q said. "And why."

"You already did," Garnier said. He wanted nothing to do with this, didn't want to hear any more of Q's ravings. "At Stark's house, the night you tried to kill his son and wife."

"If I wanted Stark's family dead, they'd be dead," Q said. His fingers did a drum roll on his knees.

"Stark and I got there in time to stop you."

"I *waited* for you. I had been there for an hour and not killed them. I was remote-viewing you. Baiting you. Just as I baited you here."

"No," Garnier said. "You got caught. Outsmarted by me and Stark."

Q snorted. "*Me*? Outsmarted by *you*? You have always held yourself in high regard. But please. Do you *ever* think? I told you long ago I was being drugged by the program. We were being used. Did you believe me? No. Because you don't think." Q tapped his forehead with a finger. "The reality is just occurring to you now."

Garnier tried to move his hands, even a pinkie or toe, but he was helpless. He looked at the window behind Q. The sun was coming in, and he heard a car go by. He was on a street—not a busy one, but not some country road either. Nor a highway. A residential area. His head ached, the pain a vise squeezing the sides of his skull.

None of what Q was saying made any difference. He had tied families to chairs and tortured them for answers they could not give, because the names he had found in Dr. Brady's files had only coincidentally borne the same names as the families he'd tracked down. They were ordinary folks who knew nothing. He had got it horribly wrong.

"You told us why you killed them and who you thought they were, and you were mistaken," Garnier said. "You killed innocent people. You *confessed* to it."

"That wasn't a confession. It was a *lie*. I took DNA from them, yes. And I shot them and smashed the backs of their skulls with a hammer. *Not* because they wouldn't respond to my 'test of their abilities.' That was a lie for Stark's benefit. I extracted from them what I extracted from you, and I covered it up with the hammer and the gunshots to their heads. I brought their DNA back to campus, to Dr. Romeau, so he could have the samples studied. Oh, and what his little elf found! It is beyond anything you can imagine."

Garnier needed to proceed with care now. Appease Q, but not pander to him either.

"What did they prove?" Garnier said. His head hurt so much, he felt he would be sick. He closed his eyes, but the room seemed to swim.

"I can't say right now," Q said.

Garnier opened his eyes. His vision was blurred, and Q's outline appeared warped. "I'm just supposed to believe that Dr. Romeau and you are, what, partners in crime? Partners in *justice*? He might be dead—murdered by you, for all I know."

Q gave a foul smile, and he knew.

"You killed Romeau," Garnier said. He felt a wave of nausea.

"His usefulness expired," Q said. "But I am telling you the truth. Those families were not human. I got their names from Dr. Brady. I forced him to tell me who I was. *What* I was. What we are."

"You killed him too."

Q shook his head as if to banish or summon a thought, and his demeanor changed. "The program is not what we thought. It never was."

He was batshit crazy, that much was clear. And Garnier was not getting out of this alive.

"I suppose you can prove it," Garnier said.

"You are not prepared to believe. There is one way, though, to know for yourself that I speak the truth."

"What way?"

"Firsthand knowledge." Q leaned in toward him, his long fingers covering his bony knees. Though he looked far healthier than he had weeks ago, he had a sour smell about him. It felt like the underlying stench of something dying from the inside out. "After I release you, find a doctor to take a DNA sample and test it. There is no one in the field of genetics who will look at your DNA and not be staggered by what they see. Be prepared for it."

"Even if our DNA was somehow . . ." Garnier could not string his thoughts together. The pain in his head was apocalyptic now. Crippling.

"Our DNA," Q said. "*Yes.* That is where the answer is. Have yours checked. You will understand then why I discontinued those *families.* Do you think what we do came naturally? Without help?"

Garnier had never understood how he could remote-view—never

grasped the mechanism. There was no explanation for it. From an objective stance, what he could do was impossible.

Garnier was about to speak, but Q silenced him, raising his palms like an evangelical preacher. "Romeau first told me about the existence of the families, out in the Wilds. A *project*. Led by Dr. Brady. Romeau thought I was advanced enough to glimpse the truth. I wasn't. He believed I would side with the program. I didn't. When Brady left, I knew he had misgivings too. When I found him in his shack in the New Mexico desert, he told me what these so-called families were."

"Human beings," Garnier said.

Q shook his head, violently. "You are naive. I can forgive you such a shortcoming. As with any child, the 'truth' the program fed us went unquestioned. There was no reason to question your ability. It would be like questioning your ability to see or walk!" Q was winded, his breath raspy.

"Tell me what you have to tell me," Garnier said. "Get this over with." His eyes stung. His brain felt molten and his head too heavy for his neck, which felt strangely brittle. His teeth ached as if their roots were suddenly rotting out.

"Get it over with," Garnier said.

Q walked around behind him.

There was the sound of a metal zipper slowly working, opening or closing.

CHAPTER 35

Stark knocked on the door of Garnier's motel room.

No answer came.

He knocked again and peered in the window but could see only the shadows of furniture.

"I'll get the manager," King said.

She returned moments later with a young woman who wore a black pantsuit, as if she were commanding the desk at a Kimpton hotel rather than a regional chain motel. Her hair was back in a ponytail, and her earrings were gold studs.

She nodded to Stark without a hello and swept her key card against the door keypad.

Apparently, King had identified herself as FBI and communicated the circumstances to this woman, and the woman was obliging them with swift, efficient professionalism.

Stark went in and searched the motel room.

Garnier was not here, and neither was his suitcase, which should be here now that he had arrived back from Maine.

Stark called him again. Nothing.

He tried to locate Garnier's phone using his own phone's tracking and syncing. He had no luck.

He called Agent Lamb at HQ.

"I need you to try to locate a consultant I'm working with. Gilles Garnier." He gave the number. "I can't get him to answer or return texts. Can't get a ping on Find My Phone."

He paused.

"All right. Good," he said.

Except that it wasn't good.

Something was wrong.

CHAPTER 36

It was raining in Concord, New Hampshire. A hard, cold, wind-driven rain. The Merrimack River was socked in.

The Valley Solar Company was located on a street along the river, among mostly renovated brick mill buildings from the 1800s.

Stark and King ducked under an awning and entered the building.

They were swiftly greeted by the company's dispatcher and its president, who showed them to a small meeting room. The walls were adorned with award certificates from the solar industry, and photos of covered bridges.

The four of them sat at a wooden table. The company president, wearing a checkered shirt and jeans, sat at the end of the table, his hands folded before him. His black beard was trimmed neat and tight.

The dispatcher, a woman with white hair and big eyeglasses, who looked to be in her sixties, took a laptop from its bag and opened it.

"What is it you need?" she said.

Stark said, "I want to make clear, we're not interested in any of your drivers in any crime, other than as possible witnesses. We just want to know where your various vans were this past Tuesday at two thirteen in the afternoon."

"Which van?"

"All of them," King said.

"Oh . . . you don't know which?" the dispatcher said.

"It's a complicated situation," Stark said.

She turned the laptop around to Stark and King. "I can get you that. All our vans are GeoTracked." She worked the keys of her laptop. "Here. We had seventeen vans out at that time. I can give you the location within twenty feet."

"What is this about?" the president said. He got up and stood behind Stark to look at the laptop screen.

"All I can say is, time is of the essence," Stark said.

"Can you exclude vans that were parked?" King said to the dispatcher. "And those on highways, interstates. We want a van that was on a street."

"Residential or commercial area?"

"Both."

The dispatcher worked the keyboard again, showed the results to King and Stark.

"That narrows it from seventeen to three," the dispatcher said. "All three were moving at the time, at a speed less than forty miles an hour. Here. See the map. These red icons of vans show exactly where they were at that time—give or take twenty feet, as I said. You can see the exact address beside them."

Three was manageable, Stark thought, though just barely.

CHAPTER 37

Q returns to the chair and sits down with a small black bag on his lap. It is shiny, like patent leather.

From the bag, he takes a steel syringe and rests it on the table beside him. Next, he brings out a shiny steel scalpel and a tiny pair of silvery pliers.

"You will understand soon," Q says. "You and I are a part of those families. Born prisoners and remain prisoners. Those people I killed provided invaluable information. I lied to you. I knew they couldn't remote-view. But they were part of a lineage in the program even if they were rejects. Beta. When I injected one of them, I saw the scar. I cut into it, and I saw what was inside. I knew it was inside me too. I can see your pain. I know it. I learned from those families. How to end it."

"But why the *kids*?"

"The kids were from the people they called their parents, yet also of the program. Part of an ugly legacy."

"I don't believe you."

"You notice I am different from when you saw me last. You can see

I am better. Healed. I feel invigorated. Fresh. Born anew. Clean. You can be too. You will be."

Q rests his hands on Garnier's shoulders and bows his head as if he were a priest praying over an ill parishioner, then steps back with a solemn look.

CHAPTER 38

"Bring up every address on your laptop," Stark said to King when they were in their vehicle again, parked in a lot across from the solar company. "Bring us into 3-D satellite so we can see all the buildings and surroundings of each van."

King brought up the first address. "The structures around it are commercial, retail, and bakeries. A fly-fishing shop. A donut shop. All are in operation. I don't think any of the buildings are right for holding someone against their will."

"Let's go through all of them. We're likely looking for a vacant building or a residence."

"Ground floor too, I presume," King said. "Garnier saw the van because the place the hostages are in must be street level. Otherwise, he'd never see the van."

"Go over all of them. Find the ones that fit."

King worked the satellite maps of each location, manipulating the 3-D and zooming in at numerous angles from the street. It took some time, but in the end, she narrowed it down to three possible locations.

"I'll get high-altitude drone surveillance out of the Bedford office on all the sites and get eyes on the buildings. We'll work with local and regional. Sit tight here until eyes are on them."

CHAPTER 39

"I need you to record it," S says to Randolph. "And you need to *mean* it. This is your chance to rectify your part in all this."

S walks in a slow circle around Randolph.

"And you'll let my family go?"

She stops in front of him. "If you mean what you say. If you just go through the motions, well . . . Do you believe what I told you?"

"Yes," he says.

"And do you genuinely want to reveal to the world what you now know to be true?"

"I do. Genuinely. I had no idea." His voice trembles. S believes him as much as she can believe anyone. It isn't much, but it will have to do.

"I'll start recording you with my phone. Collect yourself. Give yourself time to recover, for movement to return to your limbs. Do you want some water?"

"I'd like some water, yes."

S holds a cup of water to Randolph's lips. With some effort, he gets his hands around it. His movements are slow, labored. He cradles it as if it were a heavy marble chalice instead of a cheap plastic cup. He drinks until the water is gone.

"Ready?" she says.

"You'll release them? Release me?"

"I will." There is doubt in his eyes. S doesn't fault him for that.

"Ready?" she says.

"Ready."

"Go ahead."

"I am John Randolph. I am a researcher. My life's work has been in pursuit of a molecular answer for the human body to combat its own cancer. I developed a new molecule that can be synthesized to kill cancer cells and leave healthy cells alone. I want it to be a cure, and I hope one day it will be. But . . ." He stares into the camera. "I lost my way. I needed funding I couldn't find in the public sphere. I found it with a private benefactor. It is a scientist's dream to be so well funded. It allowed me to delve more deeply and swiftly into my research. It also allowed me luxuries I had never known. I had absolute financial security.

"But. I didn't do my due diligence. I didn't see the connection for my work to be used in other fields. In my research, I manipulate genes—the genetic makeup of embryos. These embryos are nonviable. They could never become actual humans. But in my haste, I let my ego get the upper hand. I took the money—a lot of it. I made more money from a few hour-long speaking engagements than I made in the previous decade. My research was used in ways I never imagined. It was used to catapult a controversial—and to my mind immoral—use of gene modification. I have come to learn that certain individuals, a certain organization I knew as the Institute for the Advancement of the Human Mind, used my research, and the research of others, to serve only themselves. For the past three decades, they worked to perfect gene editing in a way that the mainstream has not thought possible until very recently. They have already achieved it. Exceeded it. It sounds . . . it makes me sound unstable, perhaps. They have created a new subspecies of human being."

CHAPTER 40

"We've got drones on all three locations," King said as she and Stark watched the drone's video stream on her laptop. "One here." She pointed to a satellite map, zoomed in tight. "At the intersection of Bank Lane and Pierce Street in Bow, New Hampshire. Shows it's twenty minutes south from where we are now. Looks like a clapboard building in a residential neighborhood."

"We have high-altitude drone imagery and regional FBI that passed by the location in vehicles," Stark said. "Here."

The live stream showed several children playing in the front yard, pushing a tire swing and playing tag. A woman and a man, perhaps in their mid-forties, were out on the steps watching the kids play and drinking mugs of something warm. The woman went in and out the front door several times.

"Unlikely he's there," King said. "With so much traffic, people clearly living there."

"Agreed," Stark said. "But we have a vehicle with two agents at the ready, just down and across."

"The second location is on River Road, just outside Portsmouth—a town called Durham," King said. "An hour east of us. The place is vacant. That's the kind of place he'd want."

Stark brought up the live stream. "Maybe. It's vacant, but it looks gutted."

"It was the scene of a fire. The windows are blown out, the front of the building charred. But he could still have them there," King said.

"It's possible," Stark said. "There's only one way in—from the front, street side. I don't think he'd take them in that way. It's too conspicuous. I'll see that it's staked by a vehicle."

"I like the third location," King said. "A vacant storefront on Savoy Street in Keene. It was an arcade years ago, then a video store. Vacant for a decade. An hour and change southwest of us."

"No. It has to be here," Stark said, insistent. He jabbed his finger at the second location, in Durham. He zoomed in on it as he whispered, barely moving his lips. "Nod your head."

King nodded but whispered back. "Keene's the likeliest location. A quiet street too. Access is easy from the back. You don't have to go in from the front. There's an abandoned parking lot back there.

"What if he's viewing us? Right now?" Stark was whispering again. "We can't tip him off, let him see us in advance. I'm betting he can't view us and the agents at once. Can't split his attention that way. It's like trying to look in two different directions at once. Send several vehicles to Keene. Discreet."

He had a point.

King tapped a finger on the Durham location. "It has to be here."

CHAPTER 41

Q sat in the chair before Garnier, legs stretched out before him, arms folded casually across his chest.

"How's the head?" he said.

"Bad," Garnier said. It hurt to talk. It hurt to blink. The little bit of light in the dim room bludgeoned his eyes.

"I know how you feel. Side effects."

"Mmm," Garnier said.

"S," Q shouted, making Garnier jump. "S!"

Garnier heard the sound of a door opening behind him. Then footsteps.

A shadow passed across him, and S came to stand before him.

"X," she said. "He's telling you the truth."

"He's told me nothing but nonsense, that humans aren't human," replied Garnier. "He raves but can't put two coherent thoughts together."

She rolled a cart over from the side of the room. It had a white sheet covering it.

She peeled the sheet back.

Beneath it sat a shallow stainless-steel dish the size of a dipping plate. But instead of vinegar and a drizzle of olive oil, it contained what looked like a snarl of tiny translucent, oily . . . *tentacles*. That was the word that came to mind. They moved like the arms of a tiny squid that could fit in his palm, curling and uncurling, writhing and wriggling as if in their death throes. As they twisted and contorted, they went from translucent to a dark, deep red, then black. There seemed to be a sound emanating from them as well, an angry hissing like that of a threatened cat. Whatever they were, they were alive and dying.

"What the fuck is that?" Garnier said.

"That," Q said, glancing at the tiny squirming mass, "was inside me. And it's still inside you. Causing you pain. And I intend to rid you of that pain."

CHAPTER 42

King didn't like driving in the opposite direction of the target, but Stark was right: They needed to trick V if he was viewing them. Stark had three teams of agents heading to the target in Keene, all from different directions and all in civilian cars: a Jeep Wrangler, a Prius, and a Chevy pickup.

Each vehicle was equipped with a parabolic microphone, and the drones were fitted with thermal-imaging devices so the agents could tell how many people were in the structure, and where, if they were there at all.

An FBI helicopter was tracking the vehicle Stark and King were in.

If V and the hostages were determined to be inside the Keene target, Stark would be told to pull over at the nearest spot the chopper could put down. He and King would board it and could be in Keene inside twenty minutes.

Stark had been driving east toward Portsmouth for half an hour when the call came. There were five living bodies inside the Keene location.

He was ordered to pull off on the south side of the road in 3.8 miles. The helicopter would be waiting in the playing field just off the road.

When they arrived at the field, the helicopter was waiting, its blades cutting the air with a terrible racket and blowing dirt in small cyclones. A man waited for them at the open door and helped them inside. In a moment, they lifted into the air.

"We'll be putting down in a ball field a half mile away," the agent out of Bedford said into his headset microphone. "We stand ready with a car to take you to the location."

The helicopter put down in the ball field, a crowd of onlookers gawping as if this were irrefutable proof of alien life.

Stark and King were hustled to a car, ducking from the hurricane of wind whipped up by the copter's main rotor.

The agent driving pressed a finger to his earbud. "They're inside," he said to Stark.

The three vehicles sat parked at different vantage points around the location, each manned with three FBI agents ready to back Stark and King up through the rear entrance and from the sides.

Stark and King got their tactical gear out of the Prius's trunk and put it on. The women and two girls were in there. V was too. They had to be.

"They're all in a room to the left of the front entrance," the agent said.

Stark stared at the building's stick-a-brick facade, the yellowed newspaper covering the storefront windows from the inside, the FOR LEASE sign in the lower-right corner of one window.

A piece of newspaper had peeled away, leaving just enough of the glass uncovered for an eye to peek into the place—or out of it.

He realized he could really use Garnier right now, just as he had needed him the night Q took his wife and Francis hostage.

But Garnier wasn't here.

Where was he?

CHAPTER 43

"You want me to believe that you cut that out of *yourself*?" Garnier said. Even speaking hurt, the words coming out in a slow, barely articulate murmur.

S looked on, not saying anything. She had done it, Garnier knew now. She had killed those people. But she was brainwashed, duped. Manipulated into doing it.

"I didn't find it in the cupboard with the cereal," Q said. He peered at the bloodstain on the tip of his thumb.

The surgical instruments arrayed beside the tiny squirming mass on the stainless-steel tray were bloodied.

"I'll ask again," Q said. "How is your head?"

Garnier could not answer, the pain was so fierce.

"I understand," Q went on. "Not only that, but I also empathize. There is so much we don't understand. We don't even know what death is, let alone life."

"I think we know what death is," Garnier said.

"Hmmph," Q said. He turned and looked out the window, his back to Garnier.

Slowly, he turned to face him. "There is this frog," he said. "It freezes solid in the winter. Solid as rock. Imagine. Its blood freezes. Seventy percent of its body is frozen *solid*. It is as hard as a stone. Its breathing stops. Its heart stops. Its brain function stops. The frog is dead. By any and all definitions known to us today, the frog is absolutely and utterly dead. But! But but but but!" He wagged a finger.

Q was ranting now, his mind spiraling down a drain of monomaniacal nonsense. Garnier knew that the farther down the drain Q went, the more he would work himself into a violent lather, and the likelier he was to kill Garnier.

"In the spring, this frog comes back to life," Q said. "You tell me. What defines 'dead' other than zero body function, zero brain activity, zero heartbeat and zero breathing, and being frozen solid? There are two possibilities. One: Our definition of 'dead' is wrong. Lack of brain and bodily function and no heartbeat, no circulating blood, does not constitute death as we know it. Or, two: The frog *is* truly dead and is resurrected every spring. It's dead. Then it is alive." Q clapped his hands together, startling Garnier.

"We don't know *anything*! We don't know how anything works, or why. We don't even know the definition of *death*. Because, by all accepted definitions, that frog is dead as dead can be. And it comes back to life."

Q waved his hands around as if to an invisible audience that surrounded him, then slumped back in the chair before Garnier.

"We're always trying to edge forward," he said, quietly, as if half to himself. He wrung his hands, looked down at his empty palms. "Create something better than nature can. To replicate nature yet at the same time combat it. But we can't do it by natural means. We must tinker and interfere. We can't make an actual bird's wing, because we cannot create those substances, those molecules, out of nothing. We can only copy them, mimic them by cobbling together approximations with materials not even close to the original."

"What's that have to do with what we can do?" Garnier said. Q was off the rails, gone. And yet, at the center of all his ranting was a kernel of truth—something Garnier needed to understand.

"We can't do it alone." Q was sweating now. He rose to his feet and reeled, unsteady. He swayed for a moment and then paced, wiping at his mouth with the back of his hand. "That . . . *thing*." He pointed at the little tray on the cart. "It helps us remote-view. I don't know how, or even what it is. But we are nothing without it or the program. *Nothing!* We owe the program our lives. But we are not beholden to it. Not any more than a child is beholden to controlling, manipulative parents. We didn't ask for this life, this world. And what the program wants from us, demands from us, isn't natural. It isn't right. It never was. We are nothing more than a means to an end to them. That, there . . ." He pointed again at the tentacled abomination on the tray. "How do you explain what I cut out of myself?" Q said.

"How do I know you cut it out of yourself?" Garnier said. "Or if there's a thing like that in me? Even if there is, I'm still human. That thing is no more than an implant to enhance my natural potential, no different from a pacemaker or a prosthetic limb." Garnier's heart pounded in his chest so hard, he thought he might pass out.

"You doubt me," Q said. "Understandable. But you don't have much time to linger in that doubt. I've accepted it, our origin. But I don't accept what they deem to be our destiny. I will not do their bidding, and then be shut down like outmoded equipment. Do you want your ability back, or not? Do you want to live, or not?"

CHAPTER 44

Stark and King climbed the porch steps, and King hammered the door with her fist. "FBI! Open up! Warrant! Warrant!"

Stark wielded his handgun, gestured for King to try the knob.

King threw open the door and covered Stark as he entered, sweeping the front room with his weapon. The other agents stormed in from the rear of the place, shouting and identifying themselves. "FBI! Warrant! Warrant!"

They entered the large, empty front room, shaking their heads in disappointment.

The door to the next room was closed. King tried it. It was locked.

She was about to kick it down when a voice behind it said, "Please don't hurt us! Please!"

It was a young girl's cry.

With hand signals, Stark directed the agents to take up positions at either side of the door.

His fingers signed, *three . . . two . . .*

King kicked in the door.

In a corner of the room, two women and two girls cowered from the agents' brandished firearms.

The room was small; no one else was there.

"Stand down," Stark commanded.

The agents lowered their firearms.

"Are you okay?" Stark said.

Janice Randolph, the older of the two women, nodded. "Fine," she said. Her voice was calm. "Now. Yes. We're fine."

"Where is he?" King said.

"He ran out the back," she said.

Stark dashed back out of the room for the back door as someone shouted, "FBI! Down! On your knees! Down, now!"

Stark turned back to King. "Get them out of here, out the front," he said. "Get them to safety outside."

Out in the back abandoned parking lot, V was on his knees, hands zip-tied behind him.

Stark hulked over him. "Where are they?"

"I don't know who you mean," V said.

"Garnier—where is he?" Stark said.

"I don't know a Garnier."

"X. Where the hell is X!?"

V shrugged.

"Remote-view him," Stark said. "Tell me exactly where he is. It's over for all of you. You're going to wither away in prison. X. Where is he?"

V closed his eyes. "A farmhouse," he said. "In Hohenwald, Tennessee."

"Where? What road?"

"East of the town. Off Route 412. A place called Langford Hollow. The old Jorgensen place."

"That wasn't so hard to remote-view, now, was it?"

V opened his eyes. "I didn't have to remote-view. I knew. And I told you because I know it's too late. You'll never get there in time."

"And Randolph. Where is he?" Stark said. "Is he with X?"

V smiled, then made the gesture with his fingers, zipping his lips.

Stark walked over to where King was with the hostages.

"Mrs. Randolph," King was saying, "the worst is over now. You're safe."

"But *he's* not safe," the woman said. "My husband is not safe."

"We'll find him," Stark said.

"He did something to us," one of the twin girls said. "He's got Granddad, and he said they can always come back and finish the job. He said we were all going to die if Granddad didn't do something."

"And what did they want him to do?" King said.

"I don't know," one twin said.

"Probably something bad," the other twin said. "Very bad."

"We'll need statements from all of you," King said. "You'll be interviewed and debriefed. We will also provide you with crisis counseling."

Stark turned to an agent. "I need these folks taken to Bedford for debriefing, witness and victim reports, and to have them tested for whatever drugs were given to them."

"Come with me," Stark said to King. "We need to get to Logan Airport."

CHAPTER 45

As the FBI jet approached the distant carpet of lights that was Nashville, King said, "Q will know we're coming."

"There is nothing we can do about that. I have agents holding tight at the end of that road. And drone support, but either way, he'll know we're coming. I don't think he's in any position to flee. I think wherever he is with Garnier, he needs to finish it there."

King's tablet pinged. She looked at it and started reading intently.

"I have something here about the three victims. Details possibly tying them—or at least their fields—together."

"Save it. Buckle up."

CHAPTER 46

"I don't know," Garnier said when Q returned.

He wanted to rid himself of the pain and remote-view again, as he had before his ability began to disintegrate. The blinding headaches and fatigue, the dizziness and nausea. But he couldn't trust Q, or S. He couldn't trust that what was squirming and coiling on the cart came out of Q. He tried again to remote-view Stark, to get a sense whether Stark knew that he was missing, that he was in danger. He couldn't do it.

"You're wasting your time mulling it over," Q said. "I speak from experience." He picked at something between his front teeth. He made a small sucking noise. "I'll remove it. It will take time. And after, you might feel . . . strange. But you will recover, and your ability will be stronger than ever. But you must believe me. If you don't believe me, believe S."

Garnier tried again to let Q's words settle in his mind. Q was playing him to meet his own ends—ends that Garnier could not yet see. Q was a murderer and a manipulator. He was challenging Garnier to find out for himself whether he was lying.

"I might believe S," Garnier said, though he wasn't sure he could.

"Good," Q said.

Q opened a door on the wall to his left, and Garnier saw the room. Dimly lit, it had a gauzy natural light bleeding in from behind a curtain drawn on a window. A man sat in a chair. He looked much older and frailer than in the photo Garnier had seen, but Garnier still recognized him. Randolph.

S stood behind the chair. "You liked her," Q said. "Like her. More than you ever cared for me. If you and I were brothers, she was your sister, but not mine. She never liked me. But she does understand that some things in life are more important than liking one another. Some missions.

"I know you'd like to play FBI, see me taken in again to your buddy Stark," Q said. "You might see that yet. Not today, but I might even turn myself in when my work is done."

"Why would I believe that?" Garnier said.

"I'll have nothing to live for after my mission is complete. A cell the size of my room at Stargazer, three square meals, books to read, structure—it might do me some good. I've never really cared for company. Maybe I'll get lucky and get solitary confinement. One can hope.

"Until then, we must persevere. Work together. You need to get your lab work done and DNA tested and see what rises to the top. The truth always rises. Will you allow S to remove it? So you can remote-view *and* be able to leave here to get your DNA tested?"

"I'd rather die in pain than have you cut me open."

Q smiled. "Of course," he said, "you don't really have a choice."

He picked up a fresh syringe from the platter. "Just a tiny little sting and then, voilà, you wake up fit as a fiddle. And you can be on your merry way to a doctor to get that DNA profile done. We're in this together. You're smart, just a bit naive. Slow to come around. But it's time for a team effort."

Q stepped around behind Garnier.

Garnier felt the needle pierce his neck once again. He couldn't move as the scalpel's cold, sharp point was pressed into the back of his neck.

The flesh parted. He could feel the blood trickle down his spine.

The instrument sliced deeper, in a silver explosion of pain. It took all the will Garnier could muster just to stay conscious. He felt fingers and cold steel inside his neck, probing.

The room floated away from him. He felt as if he were being dangled upside down by his feet and swung back and forth in ever-higher arcs. He was going to be sick. His neck was hot.

He vomited, then fought to remain conscious as the pain slowly ebbed.

CHAPTER 47

Driving on a narrow dirt road through the dark woods of central Tennessee, Stark saw the lights of the old farmhouse through the trees. He killed his headlights as he eased his sedan next to the FBI SUV parked on the side of the road. King powered her window down as the agent in the SUV lowered his.

The agent nodded at King and Stark.

"There's four in there," the agent said. "At least, that's what we get from our intel on ground and from the drones."

Stark and King got out of the vehicle. The night was cold, moonless, and cloudy.

"How many on the other road coming in from the other side of the target?" Stark said.

"Three, but they don't go in on anything except your word. There's a back door off a low deck. Unless they have it barricaded, it should go easily, even if it's locked."

Stark nodded. The agent rolled his window up.

He and King drew their sidearms and slowly, together, advanced on the house, through the trees.

When they reached the edge of the yard, Stark hand-signaled King toward the back of the house. Then he edged over to a window at the front and peered between the sill and the bottom of the shade.

Garnier was there. In a chair.

Q stood behind him, with what looked like a scalpel in his hand.

His hands were dark with blood.

S stood at his side, holding a bright light in her hand.

Behind them, King burst in from a room in back.

Q and S turned toward her.

Stark smashed the window out and tore down the shade.

"Down!" King shouted, her handgun trained on Q.

Q slashed S's throat with the scalpel.

Stark fired. King fired.

Q fell beside S on the floor, both of them bleeding out.

Stark came in through the window.

"There's someone in the back room," King said. "Randolph."

CHAPTER 48

Garnier awoke in a hospital bed. The light was too bright, even with the shades drawn.

He sat up. The pain was gone. Vanished. His head felt clear, empty, as if a cool, fresh breeze were blowing through his mind. He waited for the pain to return, for even a shadow of it to make itself known. He feared moving his head, feared blinking—feared any sort of movement that would taunt the pain into remembering itself.

He reached a hand behind him to touch the back of his neck. He felt a roughness back there he couldn't identify.

"Sutures," a nurse said from the doorway.

"He cut me," Garnier said.

"You were wounded, yes. We sewed you up. How do you feel?"

"Fine," he said. "Really good."

It was true his head was clear, but something was wrong too. Something off. Garnier could not discern what, exactly, wasn't right. He should feel elated to be able to think clearly, to see things as they were, with his newly unencumbered mind. But he couldn't see clearly. He tried to remote-view Stark. He couldn't do it. Tried to view King, and his luck was no better. But trying didn't bring the crushing headaches either. He was not left enfeebled and sick. He was left, simply, blank. Normal. It frightened him. As much as he distrusted and disowned the program, he feared this feeling of normality.

"Do you happen to know if my superior was here?" he asked the nurse.

"Out in the hall."

Stark and King stepped into the room.

They asked how Garnier felt. "Fine," he said. "Is he—"

"They're dead. S and Q," King said.

"Why would they kill those families and those three researchers?"

"They had some . . . ideas," King said.

"Delusional," Stark said.

"I got a report that broke down what they believed, what their motive was, and why," said King. She took her tablet from her backpack and fired it up, swiped a finger across the screen. She put on her glasses and referred to the tablet's screen. "There was an overlap," she said, "that an algorithm revealed in the scientific communities each of the victims was a part of. And each of the researchers over the past decade had gone to speak at the Institute for the Advancement of the Human Mind."

"Never heard of it," Stark said.

"Our guys believe it's actually Stargazer, the program. We've pinpointed the location of Stargazer, or this institute, and are organizing a raid for the coming weeks. It needs to be strategic and disciplined. Stargazer is *not* a *government* institution. It's a *private entity*, funded by the megawealthy. We're talking one-tenth of a percent of the billionaire class. It seems the program has been working for decades in gene editing and alteration. CRISPR."

Garnier sat up. *Gene editing.* He reached for a pitcher of water on the small table beside his bed. King grabbed it for him and poured him a cup. He drank from it. The water was warm, but it quenched his thirst.

"CRISPR?" Stark said.

"*Clustered Regularly Interspaced Short Palindromic Repeats*," King said.

"Jesus," Stark said. "Explain it to me in English."

"It's used to slice specific strands of a cell's DNA to neutralize or manipulate genes and, with that, the human condition."

"Example," Stark said.

King swiped the screen, typed, brought up her research. "Let me give you context," she said. "In China, a decade ago, a scientist used CRISPR to alter three embryos. He snipped a gene that codes the HIV receptor. The women who provided the eggs didn't have HIV, but their husbands did, and they were terrified that any child they had would be born with HIV. This scientist claimed he could prevent HIV from passing to the embryo by shutting down the gene in the husbands' DNA that enabled the HIV receptor."

"Sounds like a good thing," Stark said. "How does that link to Stargazer?"

"Hear me out," said King. "This scientist. He *implanted* viable embryos into two mothers: a single embryo in the mother who provided one egg, and two embryos in the mother who provided two eggs. The embryos were *brought to term*. Those babies were the first humans ever born whose genes were manipulated as embryos. They are unnatural. They are an unnatural subspecies of human being."

Garnier listened in horror.

Stark was not sure what to make of this, or how it connected to Stargazer.

"This experiment was not just illegal and unethical," King went on. "It was immoral. The scientist cut the HIV receptors. The child, if born healthy, would not be able to have HIV. *But* those same proteins also *block* influenza and many terrible diseases, so the babies now had no defense against those. He knowingly left babies vulnerable to chronic diseases, massive infection, severe deformity, and traumatic early death."

"Jesus," Stark said.

"And. There is *no* telling what *else*. CRISPR sometimes cuts other genes not intended to be cut and isn't exact. Laws and regulations in almost every country limit its use to nonviable embryos for this very reason."

Garnier reached again for the pitcher and filled his cup, chugged down the water.

"Scientists worldwide were horrified," King said. "He'd risked the lives and health of actual humans with a procedure decades away from approval, with no evidence of its safety or efficacy. It was a massive scandal. He was jailed."

"What happened to these babies? Were they born?" Stark said.

A nurse entered the room, and King held up answering while the nurse checked the monitor beside Garnier, took a note on a tablet, and left.

"This scientist says they were born healthy and are healthy to this day," King said.

"What do the parents say?" Garnier said. "Or other doctors or scientists?"

"No one knows *who* the parents *are*. The scientist worked in strictest privacy. The parents demanded privacy be guaranteed because of the stigma of HIV in China and the risks to their children if the embryos developed abnormally. *The children themselves don't know they are experiments.*

"The scientist compares himself to the first doctor to perform IVF. That doctor was ruined for toying with *God's grand design*, but IVF has since become common, and he is now heralded as a pioneer. Granted, he conducted IVF legally. This scientist believes history will prove him a hero. But he genetically created a subspecies of humans. Those babies, kids now, if we believe they are even healthy as the scientist says, have distinct DNA. And not just them."

"What do you mean?" Stark said.

"He performed *hereditary genomics*," said King. "Those three kids, their future generations, forever, will be genetically altered. There's a CRISPR called senomic, that snips genes for diseases like sickle cell and certain cancers. It's performed today. It only affects that particular adult patient who understands and accepts the risk. It isn't passed on. But when you do it in the *embryonic* stage, it's hereditary; the offspring are of the same subspecies."

"If these kids have major complications? Mutations?" Garnier said.

"Those are passed along too. Apple and the tree."

Apple and the tree. Stark saw himself grip the hammer. His mother cower. "Don't. Please." His father, saying the other day, "I tell you this to try to protect you, as I always did." His father hadn't slain Stark's mother. Stark had, and he'd blocked it out as Francis had blocked out his own trauma. Or had he? Was he remembering right?

"Hereditary genomic manipulation is here," King said. "The only thing preventing its use is its uncertainty. But when enough research is done to prove it can be safely controlled, the human race will never be the same. We, according to current definitions, won't be human any- more. We will be playing God—with a big *G*."

"Q believed Stargazer was doing this," Garnier said. "To us. And to generations before us. The headaches. The terrible pain and debilita- tion. The scars. All of it—"

"The Intel says Stargazer has been at the cutting edge of this sci- ence and practicing it for *decades*. They could do what that scientist did twenty-five years *before* he figured it out. Maybe more. It's thought that Stargazer used it to try to create, literally, new humans. This isn't science fiction. It's what CRISPR can do. Right now. It's as real as the three of us. But as far as creating remote viewers and individuals with other traits like that, well . . ."

They're beta, Q had said. *They're not human. Not real families.*

"It was done to us," Garnier said. "To me. I never had parents. Real parents . . ."

"We don't know that," Stark said.

"Q and S believed you were one of several generations that came along and have been tweaked along the way," King said.

"Is that possible?" Stark said.

"Very. Part of the reason it's illegal to practice beyond nonviable embryos is the fear of it being used as a modern-day eugenics program done before birth."

"I *have* heard of that," Stark said. "Creating humans à la carte with traits you prefer. Blue eyes. Red hair. Athletic."

"It goes much, much further than that," King said. "It can be used to create a child with desired traits, but also to *eliminate undesirable* traits. And who chooses what *is undesirable?* And get this: not just to eliminate it from an individual, but from humankind *altogether. Forever.* Take the genes that control, say, melanin—skin color. If it's done in the embryo as a hereditary gene edit, that skin tone will never appear in the offspring of those embryos that reach adulthood. Ever again. It will be edited out. Along with any other trait the parents, *or society, or a government* deems undesirable."

"I don't know if it can be used to create abilities like you and the other Six have," King said, "but CRISPR can currently create human beings that appear normal and healthy under scrutiny but have traits that are extrahuman."

"*Extrahuman,*" Stark said.

"Right now"—King referred to her phone's screen—"CRISPR can create human beings that can go with two hours' sleep and wake as fresh as if they slept ten hours. It can create humans who feel a fraction of pain. Get your hand cut off and it wouldn't hurt any more than if you poked your wrist with a sewing needle. Add that to a human whose blood coagulates at the wound in seconds? All this can be done, *right now,* with a snip." She worked her fingers like scissors. "Snip. Done. Imagine what a society or corporation or military could do with that?"

"It can't be that easy," Stark said.

"*It is.* It can be done in a lab in forty seconds. Today. And those traits are passed along *forever.* And are irreversible. It's been possible for decades."

Garnier needed to escape this room. He felt too warm. Faint. Sick. "I thought it was cutting-edge stuff," he said.

"It was discovered in 1973. Decades earlier than is generally understood outside the most highly funded scientists," said King. "They kept it under wraps, passing it along in a very secret, hermetic society of scientists. A cabal. It wasn't publicized in 1973 because it was discovered by two women, Diane Price and Gwendlyn Goldsmith, and, well, women making such a discovery? That just would not do."

Price, Garnier thought. *Price? In the 1970s.* The same surname as

Pat Price. The former Burbank, California, police commissioner had scoured mug-shot books for the Berkeley PD and identified Don De-Freeze, aka Cinque Mtume, as the kidnapper of Patty Hearst, and he had been right. He also gave the location of the car used in the commission of the crime.

Pat Price who, a year later, met with the NSA brass to discuss remote viewing and who, a short time after that, on a trip to Las Vegas to hand off papers for safekeeping to a confidant, complained of severe cramps and died mysteriously.

That was in 1974, the year after Diane Price and Gwendlyn Goldsmith discovered CRISPR.

Was there a connection with this Diane Price?

"Q and S thought Stargazer created them, the Six, and these families," Stark said. "And wanted to stop it?"

"All of it, is my guess," King said. "Put an end to it being hereditary by killing the entire subspecies. A two-pronged effort. One: Stop those researchers and funders who, knowingly or unknowingly, contributed to the advancement of the program's ability. Two: Destroy those individuals they believed were carriers of edited genes. They believed they were doing good."

"It's insane, of course," Stark said.

"Of course," King concurred. "There is no proof whatsoever that this science is tied to their ability to remote-view. But, if they are right, a simple DNA test could prove it. And it still doesn't justify what they've done."

"You think someone who funds Stargazer was behind the actor hired to play Valken, or behind Franklin's death?" Garnier said.

"We need evidence," Stark said. "Those people are hard to get at. But Randolph can help us. He's willing to help with anything he knows. And when we raid Stargazer, there is bound to be a hoard of useful digital and physical records. That's for another day. If you even want to be part of it." Stark nodded at Garnier.

Garnier didn't know what he wanted.

CHAPTER 49

Garnier lay awake in his hospital bed, thinking over everything he'd been told, both by Q and by Agent King.

He had thought that all Q's ranting was nonsense, the ramblings of a mind that had slipped its moorings. Now he wasn't so sure. Who could explain the ability that Q and Garnier and the rest of the Six had? Garnier couldn't.

What had the program been up to all these many years?

Q had always thought he didn't remember his family because he had come to the program when he was so young. Now he believed he'd never had a family. He had been raised in the program because the program *created* him.

There was one way to know for certain.

He thought about the woman King had mentioned—one of the two female scientists who had pioneered CRISPR and were then forgotten. Price was her last name. *Price.*

Price.

Price.

Garnier didn't know what to make of it all.

But he knew one thing he needed to do.

He pressed the call button and waited.

When the nurse entered, he said, "I was wondering, how would I go about looking into a DNA test?"

"In what way?"

"Just to have my DNA sequenced—you know, for likelihood of cancers and such."

"It's easy. Just get a swab of your cheek, fill out some paperwork, and wait."

"I can do that," Garnier said.

ACKNOWLEDGMENTS

My continued thanks to everyone who has encouraged my writing, particularly my lovely and loving wife, and my daughter and son, for their smiles, hugs, and joy, and for their love of books and stories.

My thanks to everyone at Blackstone Publishing, especially to Josh Stanton for having faith in my writing to take on several books. Thanks to Stephanie Stanton and her genius that sees to it that my books' covers, and all artwork associated with my books, stand out from the crowd with striking and original design and artwork. It is an immense pleasure to know my books have the backing of such a committed and gifted team. Thank you to Executive Editor Josie Woodbridge for leading the way and shepherding this book through the editing process, and to Michael Carr, who again helped shape and improve this book in ways I never could alone.

Many thanks to Levi Coren, who fine-tuned the book with a keen eye.

This particular novel involves the FBI, about which I've never written until now. For all the details and insights on protocol and SOP, and the mindset and lives and work of FBI agents, I am indebted to career FBI agents Thomas O'Connor and Jean O'Connor for taking many hours to provide me with invaluable input that makes this book work on a level I could not achieve on my own. You were very generous with your time and information. Any errors in such matters, or liberties I took for dramatic reasons, are solely mine. Thanks also to both of you for your dedication to the law and our justice system.

On other law enforcement matters, my friend Vermont State Police Det. Sgt. Tyson Kinney has been an invaluable resource. Thanks again for the help and for lighting a fire in me to get out in the woods this past November!

Special thanks must go to Ryan C. Coleman at the Story Factory, who worked with me for countless hours on this book, and all my books. Your direction and support and good humor are invaluable.

Of course, none of this would be possible without my agent Shane Salerno at the Story Factory, who dedicates immense time and energy and talent into championing my work. My continued gratitude for all you've accomplished on behalf of my novels and for my family.